Mole Men

The strange story of a
cropduster, Mole Men, a
worm ranch and a blonde
named Ruby Falls.

Webb Wilder
Last Of The Full Grown Men

"Mole Men"
by Shane Caldwell
& Steve Boyle

Worm Ranchers Publishing LLC

Nashville

Webb Wilder, Last of the Full Grown Men "Mole Men" & "The Doll"

This book is a work of fiction. Names, characters, places and incidents are the product of the authors' sad imaginations or are used fictitiously. Any resemblance to actual places, events, things or people, living or dead, is totally and unequivocally coincidental. If this resembles your life, don't call us, call one of those tabloid television shows.

You're holding a WORM RANCHERS PUBLISHING Mystery Novelette. Now, wash your hands.

Worm Ranchers Publishing LLC

P.O. Box 58285
Nashville, Tennessee 37205
USA

ISBN: 978-1-7376675-0-6

Library of Congress Control Number: 2021916365

Second Printing 2021
First Edition 1996

for more information visit:
www.WebbWilderLastOfTheFullGrownMen.com
www.WWLOTFGM.com

COVER ART AND GRAPHICS BY
ELVIS WILSON, NASHVILLE, TN

To JoAnn, A.D. and Corey Caldwell
and straight shooters
everywhere. (SC)

To Mary, Mom, Dad, and the
LeCoat's of First Tower. (SB)

About the Authors

Shane Caldwell - Raised on an overabundance of Mad Magazine and sugary breakfast cereals, Shane achieved cult hero status by writing and starring in two popular sketch comedy series "The Sylvan Brothers Comedy Hour" and "Cuts," the latter which has won several regional and national television awards. He lives in Nashville and tries to make sure he gets enough riboflavin.

Steve Boyle - Originally from New York and now living in the outskirts of Nashville, Steve watches way too many old film noir detective movies and understands why the French like Jerry Lewis. He has been in the film and television business for over twenty years, winning over forty regional, national and international awards for his quirky music videos and commercials.

Prologue

I t was just past dark when the blearey-eyed pilot took off on his monthly strafing run. The night was clear and the full moon made like a giant streetlamp throwing an eerie light on the fields below. He had planned on double dusting the back forty even though they had just been plowed and not one seed had been planted. This was a preventive measure, he thought. Sort of posting a warning to any potential six-legged herbicidal maniacs.

He had just finished one lap around the outer edge of his strawberry field and was banking right to come in for a second pass when he saw something moving in a zig-zag motion across the far corner of the property. It was a man. A man in a business suit who ran frantically like he was being chased by the devil himself. The pilot lowered the plane to move in for a closer look. When he did, what he saw shook him to his frazzled core. There were three creatures with slicked heads, shiny skin and large glowing eyes holding outstretched arms that waved long silvery claws, pursuing their suited prey. Behind them were four more identical beings carrying a long cylindrical object that was lit up like an old Madam Leroux pinball machine and had, at one end, what appeared to be a giant corkscrew. The flier watched in terrified amazement as the three lead creatures closed in on the man who had now tripped and fallen in one of the furrows. The creatures then grabbed the man as the troop with the machine started to catch up. The pilot was so focused on the scene below that he momentarily forgot about flying, only to look up and see a line of trees coming straight at him. Without thinking he pulled back on the stick as fast and as far as he could, barely avoiding the treetops. He banked left and circled back through a thick cloud of crop dust toward the bizarre happenings below. His mind and heart were in an all-out race imagining what he might see when the dust cleared. Was it a kidnapping? A murder? He didn't know but the suspense was making his hands shake on the controls like a teenage boy reaching second base on a first date. The plane finally broke through the cloud as he looked everywhere for a sign of the attack. But all he saw was a very large, very strange, very ominous mound of dirt where the scuffle had been. The man, the monsters and the machine were gone.

ER DIGEST CLASSIFIEDS

page 87

One brown
ck German
ard that
s to the
f Gustave.
please call
55-2753.

One wife.
5'3", 110
years old.
the name
Sunshine.
-5843 with
00 reward

COVERT SERVICES

Webb Wilder Investigations
Last of the Full Grown Men.
No Case Too Small. We
Deliver. Call 555-4242.

Manny's Gun Emporium
St. Vegas Sizzling Summer
Sale. No reasonable offer
refused! Call 24 hours a
day. Ask for Manny or Al.
1771 Main Street. Call 254-

Ethel Com
We miss yo
forgiven.

ISO - SWF
Must like l
drives, f
binoculars a
practice. I
weapon tha
to be polis
pistol packin
Write Dang
Drawer #3
Vegas, F
Please ser
photo

Chapter 1

It was a hot day. Real hot. High noon on an August Tuesday in the less fashionable downtown section of St. Vegas, Florida. It was the kind of day that turned talc into tartar sauce. Whether you were standing or sitting, that wasn't a good feeling. No one knew this better than me, Webb Wilder. Although usually the cool and calm private eye, I was anything but as my six and a quarter frame squirmed uncomfortably in my torn vinyl office chair. My baker's dozen wingtips were propped up on a ring-stained desk that I had picked up at a motel fire sale as I read the midday edition of the *Daily Trombone* and tried to fight off the heat with a broken down air conditioner and a complimentary fan from Ripley's Funeral Home. "We dig you the most and we're the last to let you down." Neither helped much.

I had one hard and fast rule about my office hours. If no one called by the time I finished reading the noon paper, I bagged the day. I didn't want to waste my afternoons sitting by the phone waiting for suspicious husbands and wives to decide whether or not to call and take a chance on having those suspicions confirmed. Most would be. And most just didn't want to know.

The headline in today's edition read "Not So Rosy for Mr. Posey." The article stated that Lance Murdock, high powered real estate magnate and husband of the former Margaret Posey, daughter of the late congressman Waller Posey, was believed to be having an affair with an unidentified Latino beauty. It was reported the two had left the country for Havana under assumed names. The accompanying photograph of a half-dressed Murdock nuzzling his scantily clad traveling companion seemed to verify the story in scandalous fashion. The *Trombone* had recently criticized the questionable business practices of Murdock, who they mockingly referred to as "Mr. Posey" because of the commonly held notion that his success was entirely due to his wife's money and influence. As I pushed back my wide brimmed Resistol I wondered why a guy who seemed to have it all would risk losing everything for a little on the side. Must be the heat. Makes people crazier than outhouse rats. At the bottom of the page was a short article concerning the area's largest Fire Ant hill, discovered that morning in a strawberry field somewhere in the southern part of the county. The photo of the ant hill also contained an extreme, out of focus close-up of the farm owner, one Delton "Dusty" Norris, an eccentric local character known for his wild imagination and comically bizarre tall tales. He claimed that the mound had been created by a wandering band of subterranean monsters who had used it to bury their victims and were plotting to take over the world by planting its inhabitants into extinction. An amused police spokesman said that they had, of course, discounted this theory.

"Inquiring minds," I thought as I shook my head in disgust. I folded the paper and prepared to end what had been a waste of a morning and head out for "Taco Tuesday's" at Señor Bob's Burrito Bungalow. As I was about to toss the paper on the desk and hit the door, the phone rang. The rule was, the paper had to actually hit the desk before I could call it a day. Whoever was calling had made it just under the wire. I paused, letting the phone ring a few times before finally picking it up. Webb Wilder, last of the full grown men, played by the rules. Or at least, the ones I made for myself.

"Wilder."

"Webb Wilder?"

"The one and only. What can I do you for?"

"It's me. Dusty. Dusty Norris. You remember me, don't you?"

"Yeah. You called me about four months ago when you thought that little black rock you found in your backyard was really one of Big Foot's kidney stones. You just don't forget about a thing like that. Matter of fact, I was just reading about you in the. . ."

"Webb, you gotta get out here! You gotta get out here now! They're comin'! They're comin'! I seen 'em! They're comin' to get us all!"

"Whoa, put her in neutral. Who's coming to get us?"

"Mole Men! The Mole Men!"

"Mole Men, huh?"

"From the center of the earth!"

"Is Bigfoot with them?"

"No. It's worse than that. They're gonna try to take over. I seen 'em kidnap a man down there in my field last night when I was dustin'. They sucked him right down into the ground. I got evidence. And it ain't no ant hill like them papers say. It's an entrance to them Mole Men's underground hideout. And I'll tell you one thing, by God, if them no-earred mutants ain't stopped, they'll burrow all over this county, taking livestock, stealing babies and havin' their way with our women! And then, they'll bury us all! So you got to come out here! You're the only one who knows about this kind of stuff!"

He was right. I did possess an extensive knowledge of the paranormal. UFO's, supernatural beings, bizarre urban legends and the like. But this was out there. Way out there. So was Dusty. I was reluctant to waste my time talking to this nut, but it would be better than spending the afternoon choking down gut bombs at Señor Bob's. Those tacos were cheap on the front end, but you always paid for them later. Besides, I knew what it was like to be a party of one and I didn't want this fly boy who was wound up tighter than a miser's fist, to spontaneously combust because no one would listen to him. Even if he was out of his crop jockey mind.

"Okay, Cuz. I'll come out and look at your little pile of dirt. But do me a favor, will ya? Don't tell anyone else that I'm on my way out there. I'd hate for this to get around, you know?"

"Oh, you don't worry about that. Nobody'll know a thing. I've already sealed off the area telepathically. I'm like a Jedi, ya know."

"Well, hang on, Obi-Wan. I'm on my way."

As I put down the phone, I decided that I had been right. It had to be the heat.

Chapter 2

urning my flat black '55 Bel Air Coupe down the washed out dirt road that led to the strawberry farm, I caught sight of a figure wearing a strange looking headdress standing near the fence line. It was Dusty. As I drew closer, I could see Dusty's topper was a pith helmet covered in aluminum foil. A coat hanger was sticking out the top, bent to resemble an antenna. He was also wearing a garlic necklace and a pair of goggles with peacock feathers tied to the straps. Yeah, it's gotta be the heat. This is definitely the work of a sun-soaked mind.

I pulled up and stopped a few feet in front of the gate but before I could get out of the car, Dusty ran over to the open window on the passenger's side, leaned into the car and began raving and flailing like Barney Fife on a caffeine binge.

"Thank the Lord above you made it here safe, Webb! I was worried one of 'em might've got you on the way here. You gotta see it! You gotta come and see it! Then you'll believe me! It was Mole Men that done it! I'm tellin' you. It was Mole Men! With big bugged out eyes and razor-sharp claws that could cut right through petrified rock with one swipe! And they're gonna get us all if they ain't stopped!"

"Steady yourself there, Lindbergh. Now, where's this mountain of a molehill you're talking about?"

"It's right over that rise. I'll take you to it. But you better gird your psyche for a mind bendin' phenomenon."

As we went through the gate, I gave Dusty the once over. With his whacked-out wardrobe, he was a ridiculous sight to be sure and I couldn't resist hearing the reason for his unconventional accessories. I might regret it, but I had to ask.

"What's up with the lid?"

"You mean my hat? Well, them Mole Men, you see they're like bats. They can't see too good being that they spend most of their time under the ground diggin' and what not, so they have to send out them sonic waves like bats, so they'll know where they're goin'. Well, they ain't goin' nowhere near me cause this hat here will send 'em to bedlam."

"What about the garlic neckerchief?"

"That's in case them Mole Men are like them bats in other ways."

"What do you mean?"

"Vampires."

"Ah. Of course. How silly of me."

The two of us made our way across one strawberry patch, climbed another fence and finally entered the field where the huge mound stood.

"There it is. See it?" Dusty was filled with a mixture of pride and nervousness. "Now, you tell me a bunch of ants made that!"

It was indeed a large, well-formed swell of earth. About ten feet high and twice as much at its base. I did have a hard time believing that an army of ants, even a whole brigade of Giant Peruvian Fire Ants, could have built something like this. But I had an even harder time believing it was done by Mole Men. As we moved closer to the hill, Dusty hesitated.

"I don't think we should get too close. One of 'em might jump out on us and rip our guts out!"

"You wait here then. I'm gonna get a closer look."

"You want some foil for your hat?"

"No, thanks. It'll clash with my tie."

I walked to the mound and circled around it. Except for the size of the thing, there was nothing unusual. No tracks. No sign of a struggle. No ants or giant vermin droppings either. And the footprints that were there most likely belonged to the reporters that had come to take pictures that morning. I looked it over, trying to come up with an explanation of how it got there. One that would satisfy my own curiosity while easing Dusty's Mole Men McCarthyism. It wouldn't be easy.

"You know, Hoss, this thing was probably made by a bunch of mutated chipmunks. With all the chemicals you've been spraying out here, it's a wonder we don't have giant spiders roaming the countryside and forty-foot winged lizards swoopin' down and carrying off double-wides."

"You seen them too?"

"No. I'm just trying to tell you that whatever

made this wasn't some creature out of a low rent monster movie. It was an animal. Or the wind. Or a bunch of kids pulling a prank. It was something but it wasn't Mole Men. Mother Nature works in strange ways, but not that strange. Of course, on the other hand, you could be the exception."

"Well, I'm tellin' you that it wasn't no ants nor chipmunks nor any bunch of punk kids! It was Mole Men 'cause I seen 'em with my own eyes!"

Dusty paced back and forth with his hands shoved deep in his pockets, snorting and kicking dirt clods in aggravated frustration over me doubting his story.

"Hell, Webb, I thought you'd be the one person who'd believe me. I mean, I know most people think I'm a few bubbles off level, but you never treated me like that. You listened to me. And I'm tellin' you the God's honest truth -- I saw what I saw. I'll swear to you on the family Bible!"

If you pushed the right button, I could be a soft touch. Dusty, with his pathetic plea for understanding, had just hit "pity" on the Webb Wilder emotional keyboard. I had to try and help the guy out now. Guilt had proved an uncomfortable fit for me in the past and I didn't feel like trying it on again. Sadly, Señor Bob's brand of Montezuma's revenge was starting to sound good about now.

"Look, man, it's not that I don't believe you. I'm just playing Devil's advocate. You know, trying to look at it from all sides. I tell you what. I've got a friend over at Bing's Bull Dozier Barnyard who owes me a favor. I can come out here tomorrow with a backhoe and we'll dig up this heap and see what's under there. Okay?"

"What we'll see is Mole Men! Great big ones! I'm goin' back to take the plug out of my twelve gauge and lock and load. I'll see you out here tomorrow!"

I watched as Dusty scampered across the field, jumping the fence and making his way to the farmhouse to prepare for tomorrow's mole hunting mission. I looked back and gave the hill a final once over and was about to turn and go when I spied something embedded in the mound's dirt. Something that had caught a piece of the sun and was shining like a light house beacon onto my wire rims. I reached down and picked it up to see it was a long metal object that resembled a claw. For a split second I wondered if Dusty might have been right about the Mole Men. But when I saw "Forged in Cleveland" stamped on one side, I figured it was just a piece of broken plow and slipped it in my pocket and started back to my car. If this belonged to a Mole Man, he was a long way from home.

Chapter 3

I took a right onto the main road that had led me to Dusty's farm. This would take me in the opposite direction of the city, but I felt I needed a ride in the country. It would clear my head. Give me time to think. Think about Dusty and how lonely it must be when you're considered the town crackpot. I knew something about loneliness. As a young child possessed of the mind of a full grown man, I had been an egg headed outcast who found comfort in Sgt. Rock comics and Freddie & the Dreamers records, so I felt a certain kinship to this ostracized farm boy. Although, not one I would claim in public.

As I drove, the roadside scenery, which consisted mostly of power lines and the occasional fruit stand, passed by as a subconscious blur. But then, sprouting out of a grove of sprawling trees was a strange-looking billboard urging motorists to "Worm Your Way Into His Heart With a Gift Pack From Worsham's Worm Ranch."

At the side of the ad was an enormous three dimensional can of worms from which a grinning, chubby cheeked, middle aged man was bursting forth, wearing a bright red jacket and holding two handfuls of giant wriggling earthworms. The worms themselves seemed to be made out of canvas covered springs and were gently swaying in the breeze. There was also a caption at the bottom of the sign. "Visit our gift shop. One mile ahead." Creepy, but effective.

My curiosity had been peaked by this highway hard sell, so I decided that I would stop in and take a look. What the heck, maybe they had a two headed slug in there. Or a Mexican jumping worm. Or at least some of those goofy travelogue post cards that my Uncle Frank in Speonk liked so much. Anyway, it was worth a look.

The gift shop wasn't what I expected. I had pictured a cheesy little souvenir store like Rupe's or Cement Land. The kind of roadside rip-offs that advertise such amazing attractions as two-headed goats or colossal alligators, the sort of thing that aggravates and entertains you for miles along the highway, but when you finally get there, the goat's packed in a jar like gefilte fish and the alligator is made out of concrete. Tackiness abounds. But this place wasn't like that at all. It was a small, antebellum style cottage with white columns, green shutters and a couple of porch swings. Sort of like a miniature Tara. Behind it were acres and acres of black fields. Rich, dark soil that stretched farther than the eye could see. Worm dirt. If Scarlet ate red wigglers, she would definitely never go hungry again.

As I entered the store, I realized that the outside had been a facade. The inside of this little worm boutique looked more like a bait shop. Tastefully done maybe, but still a bait shop. There were rods and reels and lures and nets hung from the ceiling and walls partially hiding an old chalkboard that had scratched on it, *Happily Managed by Thelma and Jasper Newby*. There was even a little bar and grill in the back with a gum smackin' waitress running the counter. But mostly, there were boxes and boxes of custom-made worm cartons stacked high and deep beside two huge bins that were filled with dirt, and presumably worms. The boxes were labeled as worm ranch gift packs and featured a picture of the same guy that was popping out of the worm can from the roadside billboard. Leering behind the grill counter was an even larger portrait of the same guy. This, an elaborately framed, stately pose in which one hand was lifted toward heaven while the other was raised to his chest, both filled with fat red night crawlers. Above this distinguished image was a banner that read, *Welcome to the World Famous Worsham's Worm Ranch. All Worms Locally Raised and Specially Bred by Our Founder Wendell Worsham.*

I strode to the counter and bellied up, drawn by the smell of frying burgers. I knew every truck stop and greasy spoon in seven states and considered myself an aficionado when it came to road food. I figured I'd give Thelma a chance to please my discerning palate.

"Hidee, mam'. How are your burgers today?"

"Same as they are every day, hon. Good enough to make you slap your mammy."

"Well, I don't figure on seeing mine till Christmas. Think it 'ill wear off by then?"

"Just barely. Can I fix you one, dear?"

"Make it two. One for the road. It'll help me

steer."

As the kindly grease-slinger prepared the burgers, I spotted cousin Jasper in a side room digging in another bin of worm dirt. He was elbow deep, sifting and turning so far down in the tank for worms that his hands and forearms disappeared in the peat. He nodded hello and I tipped my hat, watching him work for a bit before turning my attention back to Thelma who was flappin' her gums while flippin' the patties.

"Yep. Wendy's and McDonald's got all tore up a while ago when folks said they used worms in their burgers. But we're proud if it here. They're just full of vitamins and protein. And a cow can't even come close to the taste. You'll see. You'll gobble 'em down just like a freshwater carp."

"Those are worm burgers?"

"One hundred percent! Freshly ground by Jasper, this morning."

I winced and swallowed hard. "Why don't you just make both of those to go."

"Sure, hon. I know how it is with you travellin' men when you think you've got a buyer waitin' on you. Got to get on down the road, don't you?"

"No. Back to the city. I'm not a salesman. I just came out to take a look at that ant hill over at the Norris place."

"Oh yeah. I heard about that. What are you? Bug inspector or somethin'?"

"Private Investigator, ma'am. Dusty called me to see if I could help him figure out what made that big drift in his field."

"Well, from what I hear, it sounds like he shoulda called one of them psychiatrists to help him figure out what made him lose his mind."

Thelma shook her head and turned back to the grill, continuing her evaluation of Dusty's mental state.

"Mole Men! I always knew that boy was curious acting, but this time he's gone and dove off the deep end into an empty pool. I mean, have you ever heard of anything so ridiculous in your life?"

"Yeah. Pet rocks. Ishtar. Hendrix opening for the Monkees. . . "

"You don't believe that foolishness he's talking, do you?"

"No, but just to show him there aren't any Mole Men or monsters or Commies or anything else out there, I'm coming back tomorrow with a backhoe to dig that mound up. Maybe that'll settle him down for a little while. . . or at least till I can drive away."

"You're gonna dig it up? Well, that seems like an awful lot of trouble to go to just to satisfy a goose like Dusty. If I was you, I'd just let it be. Them fellas with the white coats will be comin' for him soon enough anyway. You ought to save yourself the trouble."

"Oh. It's not that much trouble. Besides, finding your place was a nice surprise. Who knows what I'll find when I come back tomorrow."

By now Thelma had wrapped up the worm burgers and handed them to me. The bag was already soaked with grease and was starting to drip on the counter. As she wiped up the small puddle of bait butter, she looked up at me with a downhome sweet waitress smile.

"Well, if those treat you right, come on back and I'll whip you up some more. I'll make 'em double deckers the next time! Just ask for Thelma. That's what they call me. By the way, I never did catch your name."

"It's Wilder. Webb Wilder."

"Nice to have met you, dear. You come back and see ol' Thelma, ya hear?" "It'll be my pleasure, ma'am"

I tipped my hat and was turning to go when she called out.

"You forgot your burgers, hon!"

A sick smile came to my face as I picked up the sack of slime.

"Thanks. I sure would've hated to have left those."

As I slapped down the money for my bill and wheeled to leave, the beer bellied Jasper who was digging for worms in the next room looked up and grinned. I politely waved goodbye. Jasper pulled his hand out of the tank to return the wave. When he did, I could see that he was wearing Stevedore gloves. The kind made out of thick brown leather. The kind with long silver claws on the end of the fingers. The kind with "Forged in Cleveland" stamped on them. The kind I found in Dusty's ant hill. I froze stiff as the big guy waved the big clawed hand at me. Maybe Dusty wasn't so crazy after all. Maybe something strange did go on in that strawberry field last night. Maybe I'd have to find out exactly what it was. Thelma's voice broke the spell.

"You forget something, dear?"

"No just remembering something," I stuttered as I made my way quickly out the door.

Thelma watched as my car pull out of the lot and on to the highway. Unfortunately she also watched as a grease-soaked bag flew out of the driver's side window like a shot out of a cannon. The second I was out of sight, the kindly smile on her face turned cold as stone.

She picked up the phone and dialed quickly. The call was answered on the third ring.

"Wormy, it's Thelma. You've got trouble. Some long-legged cowboy detective named Wilder just left here. Says he's comin back tomorrow to dig up the mound over at that half-wit's farm. You know what he's gonna find. You better do somethin' quick."

"Don't worry, Thelma. I'll take care of it. I always do."

The voice on the other end of the phone belonged to Wendell Worsham.

Chapter 4

Though confident in tone when responding to Thelma's warning, Wendell "Wormy" Worsham was clearly agitated by the news of my plans for excavation of his crackpot neighbor's land.

As Wormy paced in front of his desk, this thick, round, ruddy-faced man with caterpillar eyebrows and a toupee so bad that it made Rip Taylor's look natural, pinched the bridge of his nose and considered what had to be done.

Wormy's moniker had been hung on him at an early age and proved to be a source of ridicule until, like a "Boy Named Sue" he turned it into a source of strength. He was considered, far and away, the largest producer of earthworms in the Western hemisphere. His worms were renowned for their high quality and unmatched effectiveness in landing the big ones. Professional bass fishermen traveled for miles to get them, and during tournament time orders from around the country flooded in, all to secure a box of Wormy's prize winning bait. And it wasn't only the pros who had used them. Just about anyone who had ever baited a hook had done it with a "Worsham Worm."

It had long been a secret as to how Worsham's Worm Ranch was able to produce such superior specimens and it was one Wormy kept to himself. Not that there were any clandestine operations like "Wormgate" planned in order to discover the mystery, but people did wonder. There was even a group of biologists from the local junior college that came out to test the soil for mineral content but Wormy refused, saying that it would interrupt the seasonal mating rituals of his "livestock." When the scientists protested, pointing out that earthworms are asexual annelids that perpetually reproduce despite minor disturbances and that his reasoning would prevent them from ever conducting their research, Wormy's half-smiling reply was "Exactly." So they left. Never knowing the real reason Wormy wouldn't allow their tests. Never knowing what Lance Murdock had known. That beneath the dirt of that farm, beneath all eight hundred acres, was an element so rare, so powerful and so unique that modern science didn't even know it existed. But Wormy knew. He called it Vermillite.

During the late nineteen forties through to the mid nineteen fifties, the government conducted rocket experiments near the site that would eventually become the Worm Ranch. As different launchings failed, their rocket carcasses were dumped with a mix of liquid and solid fuels along with loads of other radioactive experimental propellants, creating fallout more dense than any atomic contaminants caused by testing done in Utah around that same time. The land was then sealed off and quarantined for seven years, but after tests showed that the pollution levels had surprisingly dropped to safe standards, the property was sold at auction. The highest bidder was Wendell Worsham, a young bright-eyed twenty-four-year-old agriculture major, fresh out of Radley A&M. He was full of wild ideas and even wilder dreams of building an earthworm empire on his newly acquired acreage. But not even in his wildest could he have imagined the good fortune that would come his way thanks to the combination of red clay and Red Scare. Due to the presence of massive amounts of a mineral known as Vermiculite, the granules expand greatly when brought in contact with a mix of propellants and radiation, thereby producing a lightweight, highly water-absorbent material, that was absorbed quickly into the soil. The fouling of the Vermiculite formed a radically dense and unstable new element. Over the next few years this mutant mineral seeped deeper and deeper into the undisturbed ground, finally hitting the water table where it expanded at an incredible rate and began rising back up through the earth and rock, transforming everything in its path into soppy, rich, fertile layers of soil.

This new sci-fi soil acted like a grub-pumping steroid, creating a super race of Über worms. Vermis that were not only abnormally large and meaty, but could multiply at over forty times the rate of normal larvae. Thus was born Vermillite, and with that, the slithering kingdom of Wormy Worsham.

It was purely by accident that real estate wonder agent Lance Murdock had discovered Vermillite's existence. In the process of closing a deal on a farm that shared a common boundary with the worm ranch, Murdock performed a ground test to makes sure the land would percolate. It was a standard procedure in real estate transactions, like a termite inspection. . . or exorcism, except that it involved a little dirt drilling. What wasn't so standard this time were the results. In the course of the testing, water rose up from the ground like Jed's bubblin' crude, forming a small puddle around the fence line. This wasn't unusual. They occasionally struck water when drilling so Murdock paid little attention and even less to his dog Pete who was drinking from the puddle. He usually took the dog with him on these trips, ostensibly to let him enjoy the outdoors. In reality, because the hound was so near death's pet door, Murdock always hoped Pete would kick while out in a field where he could just leave him and not have to deal with a weepy backyard family funeral and the accompanying stench that went along with it. But after finding the dog the next day running and jumping like a puppy, Murdock wouldn't have taken a million dollars for the pooch. He almost didn't recognize his own dog. Pete's coat was full and shiny, and his eyes were bright and clear as he bounded around the fenced-in yard, wagging and barking with an almost uncontrollable energy. What could have caused this to happen? What could have transformed this decrepit old canine into an astonishing Rin Tin Tin? Then Murdock remembered the water at the farm. The dog had lapped it up like mother's milk. There was no other explanation. No, he wouldn't take a million for that dog. He was going to make a thousand times that because of the thirsty old mutt. No longer would school children have to remember the name

Ponce deLeon. Instead they would remember the name Lance Murdock. The guy who found the real Fountain of Youth.

Murdock immediately falsified the perc test reports and had the land declared unsound for building, allowing him to step in and snatch the farm for a song. He then obtained a geological survey of the area showing were the underground water was located. What he saw didn't make him happy. Most of the water lay beneath a tract of land next to his newly acquired piece of property. Under Worsham's Worm Ranch.

Large offers were made to Wormy for his acreage. He refused them all. Murdock tried to wheedle and cajole the eccentric bait baron into abdicating his throne but Wormy wouldn't budge. Murdock finally reached his boiling point and confessed the reason he wanted the land. He told Wormy that he knew all about the miracle water under his ranch and nothing was going to stop him from getting it. If Wormy didn't sell, Murdock said that he would be forced to slant drill and pump all the water out, leaving the worm ranch high and dry. Upon hearing this, Wormy slowly rose from his chair and pointed Murdock toward the door, coldly telling him to get out. Murdock turned to leave saying contemptuously that he had given Wormy his chance.

The favor wouldn't be returned.

Wormy's plan to kill Murdock would have come off without a hitch if it hadn't been for Dusty. And now, he brought in a detective to investigate the scene. Wormy knew he had to stop us. Both of us. He continued pacing private wormwood paneled office and began a flailing soliloquy as to how he would do just that.

"Murdock thought he was gonna take the milk

from my babies, but he didn't know how far a father would go to protect his children. Now, that fool Norris has brought in some hat-wearin' hack to try to explain what his powder brain saw last night. Well, I can't afford to have either one of those fools out there snoopin' around. Not now."

Then a light bulb of an idea went off under his worm-eaten wig.

"And they won't, 'cause somethin's gonna happen to impede this little investigation. Somethin' that's gonna make that gangly city boy detective and his monkey-brained sidekick wish that they'd never stuck the first toe out in that field."

Wormy's eyes held a demented glow as he moved toward a large, elaborately decorated tank filled with slithering worms. Breathing heavily and shaking with anticipation, he reached into the tank and brought out two wriggling handfuls and lifted them up like an Appalachian snake handler. He spoke assumingly to his "children."

"Fear not little ones. I will protect thee."

He held the worms to his face and began kissing, caressing and cooing to his slimy serpentine friends. This nauseating show of affection was accompanied by a soft, demented lullaby as Wormy drifted into a hypnotic vermicular trance.

"The worms crawl in, and the worms crawl out
    In your stomach and out your mouth
    The ones that go in are lean and thin
    The ones that come out are fat and stout
    Your eyes fall in and your teeth fall out
    Your brains come tumbling down your snout
    Be merry, my friends, be merry. . . "

Chapter 5

I had just finished sucking down the last noodle from a can of Chef Big Boy I had heated up on a hot plate I kept in the bottom right hand drawer of my office desk. I had opened the can with the "Forged In Cleveland" claw. As I twirled the claw between my thumb and forefinger, catching the light from a dangling overhead bulb, I was still confused about what had taken place that morning between the strawberry farm and the worm ranch. Sure, Dusty's story of murderous Mole Men by itself seemed about as believable as a Reverend Ike sermon, but there were too many other things to consider. How had this menacing piece of metal found its way into a freshly made mound of dirt? How had it roamed from the neighboring worm ranch to Dusty's strawberry farm if it hadn't traveled on the end of a gloved hand? Whose hand was it and what was it doing there? And why, during what had seemed before an innocent conversation, had Thelma Newby tried to courage me from digging up Dusty's Fire Ant hill? I was trying to sort it all out when my office door gently swung open.

With the light from a hallway window shining through a sheer silk skirt silhouetting two long, luscious legs that pedestaled a shapely torso draped with flowing hair cascading from under a wide brimmed summer hat, I deduced that the figure standing in my doorway was most likely. . . a woman. But not like any woman I had ever seen before. The sight sent me stuttering, "C-c-can I help you?"

"Webb Wilder?" asked the figure, her face still hidden in the backlight.

I awkwardly nodded as I stood up to walk to the front of my desk. The lady caller moved from the doorway into a more visible spot in front of my office. Now in plain sight, there was no doubt about it. She was definitely a woman. About as much a woman as a woman can be. Long, blonde hair framed perfect features. Her stunning green eyes pierced mine as her full, pouting lips moved to speak.

"I read your ad in the back of Danger Digest. 'Webb Wilder, Investigations. Last of the Full Grown Men. No Case Too Small. We Deliver.' You sound like just the man I need."

I leaned back stiffly on the front edge of my desk. With a severe case of spontaneous dry mouth, I delivered what I thought was a cracked but witty retort. "Oh?"

The magnificent creature moved closer, slowly and sensually sliding into one of the two chewed, ratty chairs that sat in front of my desk. She made it look like a throne. She crossed her smooth, tanned, well-formed legs and introduced herself.

"My name is Ruby Falls. Have you ever heard of me?"

"Only what I've read in the society pages. You're Ruby Falls, millionaire. You own a mansion and a yacht."

"I am and I do. In fact, my yacht is part of the reason I've come to see you. I'm being blackmailed by a sleazy fishing boat captain named McCreedy. He has some rather compromising pictures of me sunbathing au naturale with a cabin boy on the deck of the Squalid Opulence. That's my yacht. I christened it myself. What do you think?"

"It fits."

"Well, what doesn't fit is this slimeball McCreedy, not in my plans anyway. He says he wants one hundred thousand dollars for the negatives or he'll send them to every wire service in the country, including the *Daily Trombone*, and I can't have that happen. I mean, a woman shouldn't be punished just because she has certain needs. Hot, primal needs that she has to satisfy to keep her from writhing in unfulfilled anguish and desire. You can understand that can't you?"

With a trembling voice, I replied, "Oh, yeah."

"Anyway, I've struck a deal with McCreedy. I don't like it but I'm giving him the hundred thousand for the pictures. I told him that my brother Ralph would meet him tonight at the Cochon Bay Pier fishing office to make the exchange. The problem is I can't ask Ralph to do it. He's a little too delicate for this kind of sordid business. You know, debate team and chess club at Brockton University was about it for his extracurriculars. The other reason is that I don't want him finding out that his sister sometimes indulges herself with the hired help. So, I was wondering, could I hire you to pose as my brother and get those pictures for me?"

"Sounds pretty cut and dry."

I loosened up a bit after listening to the story of the blackmail scheme and was starting to get the feeling back in my fingers as they unclenched from the edge of my desk.

"This kind of thing is standard fare in my business. I'll get the negatives for you. I also get two hundred dollars a day plus expenses."

"You get those pictures and my money back, Mr. Wilder and I'll double your fee. Plus, I'll be very, very happy. So will you."

The sultry beauty rose out of her chair, walked behind my still half-leaning, half-standing pose and pulled out a packet of photographs. She wrapped her arms around my neck and flipped through the photos in front of my chest.

"I guess if you're going to rescue my pictures, you need to see what they look like."

Look, indeed. My eyes widened behind my steamed-up lenses as if I'd just been given an ocular enema. They were quite impressive images. It was obvious that Ruby was proud of her natural gifts as she smiled self-admiringly while displaying her attributes. I, on the other hand, sweated and shook like a tart at a tent revival.

"What's wrong, Mr. Wilder? It's hard for me to believe that in your line of work, you've never seen pictures of a naked lady."

"Oh, I've seen 'em. Just not of any that they were alive and well and leaning on my shoulder and breathing down my neck."

Putting the pictures away, Ruby pulled out an envelope and slid it inside my suit jacket pocket, patting it softly into place. I looked at her nervously, braced for whatever shock might come next.

"There's four hundred dollars in there. I'm giving you the entire fee now. Bring back the pictures and the money and you'll also have my unbridled gratitude."

"Thanks for the confidence, ma'am. I aim to please."

Walking out the door, she turned and smiled, "So do I."

Chapter 6

It was 9 p.m. I was at the front office of the fishing warehouse on the pier, disguised as Ralph and ready to meet Captain Jack McCreedy. The place was dimly lit and sparsely furnished. As I cautiously entered through the doorway, I felt a little out of place with my hair slicked back, dressed in a lavender Buddy Love tuxedo and sporting a pencil thin novelty store moustache. The briefcase filled with a hundred thousand dollars' worth of hush money was the one thing that helped me maintain my manly senses. I swayed to the center of the room and waited. A light came on behind me and I turned to see a man sitting at a desk smoking a cigarette, his darkened face escaping the glow of a gooseneck table lamp. After taking a long drag, he exhaled and spoke.

"You the brother?"

"I most certainly am," I said with a lilting lisp. "Are you the swine who has those vile pictures of my sister?"

"That's right, fancy boy. I've got 'em right here."

"And I've got the money. So, let's expedite this unpleasant transaction before I become even more nauseated standing in this tacky little crackerbox of an office smelling your fishy B.O."

"Fine with me, Alice. You give me the money. I give you the pictures. Tit for tat or I guess in this case, tat for tit. Huh?"

"Let's get on with it, shall we? And please, spare me your asinine witticisms."

"Don't push your luck sissy boy. I've got half a mind to split your skull."

"It takes half a mind to resort to such violence. Are we making a deal here or what?"

"Let's do it, then."

With that, McCreedy slowly pushed a manila envelope halfway across the desk, stopping his hand and holding out the other, palm up.

"The money?"

I lifted up the briefcase and was lowering it towards McCreedy's outstretched hand when the burly Captain's grinning, stubbly face hit the lamplight.

"Hey, swish. How does it feel to have a slut for a sister?"

The Captain's crude comment gave me an opening. While McCreedy waited for a reaction to his insult, I quickly grabbed the pictures and swung the briefcase at his head, knocking him to the floor. I turned to run but McCreedy tackled me from behind and we both went crashing into a rickety wall of shelving filled with boxes of fishhooks that went flying onto the office floor. The two of us slid down the wall and hit the ground, wrestling and rolling while being stuck like whale bait by the hooks. We quickly got to our feet. McCreedy, who had two free hands, started burrowing in, throwing Joe Frazier hooks to my breadbasket. With my hands full, I wheeled away from the body shots and stepped back into a Chevalier stance, a basic movement of Savate, the French art of Foot Fighting. Although not a devotee of a culture whose national delicacy is a fungus harvested by a snout rutting sow, I would employ their mode of combat if the situation arose. And it had. Right in my face. McCreedy moved in and threw a high hook to my head. I countered with a spinning Crossiant kick that hit McCreedy in the knee just as his punch caught my cheekbone. We both went down. While shaking out the cobwebs and still holding on to the briefcase and pictures like a terrier with lockjaw, I saw McCreedy in the doorway unsteadily getting to his feet. I jumped and ran toward him, executing a perfect Flying Souffle to the sternum that sent him out the door, over the pier rail and into the water below.

I moved to the rail and looked down to see McCreedy jerkily dog paddling toward a rusted metal ladder bolted to the pier. Not caring to wait and see if the fight had gone out of the seedy Captain, I made my hobbling exit with the stills and the bills firmly in hand.

L ying on a metal framed bunk in my dark, dank, run-down flat, I was still in my Ralph disguise nursing a bump on my head with a towel filled with ice scraped off the sides of my glacierized refriger-ator freezer. The envelope containing the blackmail pic-tures sat on top of the briefcase which rested on my stomach as I stared at the local news on a small black and white TV.

A helmet-headed anchorwoman intro'd a story concerning the Murdock Development Corporation and its errant chairman of the board, Lance Murdock. I half listened as they repeated the same information that had been in the paper earlier that day, but I gave my full attention when a familiar image appeared on the screen. It was the worm rancher. He was holding a press confer-ence castigating Murdock for his lack of morals by leav-ing his family for the delights of a Cuban beauty, to shack up in Havana. With Margaret Posey Murdock standing at his side, Worsham spoke of her fallen husband.

"It's a sad day for our community when a formerly upstanding citizen gives in to the vile temptations of the flesh and forsakes family, friends and responsibility to wallow in the mire of salacious corruption. It is even more disheartening when a sweet flower of a woman, such as this precious blossom to my right, is left behind to maintain and endure in the wake of this deplorable act of lust run amok. It is for this reason that I, following the example of the Samaritan, have offered my services to run the Murdock Development Corporation while she copes with this unpleasant situation caused by her soon-to-be-former spouse's loathsome indiscretions."

Wormy then brought the distraught Mrs. Murdock forward and placed his arm comfortingly around her shoulder.

"Rest assured, my friends. I will personally see to it that the business continues to prosper and that this fair lady shall not be further tainted by this unfortunate experience."

As the news story ended, I watched intently as Wormy turned and smiled at his new business partner while his hand moved from her shoulder and descended to a lower part of her anatomy. I was still shaking my head in bewilderment when the phone rang. It was Ruby.

"Webb? It's Ruby. Well," she sighed, "how did it go?"

"It went," I groaned, as I winced and readjusted my homemade ice pack.

"You got the pictures then?"

"Got 'em."

"And the money?"

"Ditto."

A shrill squeal pierced my swollen head like a marching band on a hangover morning. I held the phone at a safe distance until the noise subsided.

"Oh, sweet baby! You are everything your ad said and more! You really do deliver!"

"I don't believe in false advertisement. And from the way you were dressed in my office today, neither do you."

"We've got to go out and celebrate. I feel like blowin' this town wide open tonight. Bring the pictures and the money and meet me at the Blue Pelican in one hour, okay? And baby? If you like the way I was dressed today, well . . . wear glasses. You'll need 'em. Ciao."

I put down the phone, walked to the refrigerator and put my ice pack back in the freezer. From the way Ruby talked, it sounded like I might have a few more bumps and bruises to attend to before the night was over.

Chapter 8

The Blue Pelican was known around town as a pretentious snob-atorium that catered to the city's freaks and filthy rich. In reality, it was an old warehouse whose renovation consisted of bringing in tablecloths and throwing up a bunch of neon to draw attention away from the faded brick walls and rusted ceiling fans that squealed when they turned like frontier wagon wheels. But that was also part of the appeal of the place. Chic trash or trashy chic. Either way, it brought them out. And, as I stepped off the freight elevator that served as an entrance to the club, I saw that, tonight, they were out in force.

I walked over to the long bar that ran almost the entire length of the back wall, ordered a bull shot, then turned and leaned against the rail amongst the crowd of booze swilling jerks and began surveying the scene. The main floor had three levels. In the center was a dance pit stocked with flailing, gyrating bodies full of narcissism and designer drugs. The next level rose about three feet up from the dance floor with small, round cocktail tables packed in among a collection of palm and rubber tree plants. The third level was separated from the second by a circular banister and was filled with big tables of big parties with big money.

It looked like feeding time at the zoo. The place was buzzing with white coats kowtowing to the hip folk. I could never live in Funky Town, but I don't mind visiting once in a while. I downed the rest of my drink and began searching the room for my date. Then, I noticed that all the heads at the bar had turned toward the door. I looked over and saw why. Ruby had just walked in.

Every eye in the place followed her as she moved seductively across the dance floor. The crowd parted like vassals bowing to the queen as she moved through them with a subtle writhe, wearing a tight, low-cut red mini-dress that was poured on her like a can of glossy Dutch Boy. My chin was on my chest as she walked straight to me. Taking my hand and whispering, "Baby, you are sooo good," she let a wisp of hot breath flow over my ear, then softly bit the lobe and led me to a table. On the way, I took out my handkerchief, stuffed it in a glass full of ice water and drippingly wiped my face. Like Ripley's Funeral Home fan, it didn't really help.

Just as we sat down, a waiter pushing a portable bar cart, stopped at our table.

"Good evening, sir. What will you and the lovely lady be drinking this evening?"

"I'll have a bourbon, neat, no back. And the lady will have a. . . gin fizz?"

The table candlelight danced in Ruby's eyes

as she leaned in, staring at me.

"Gin's for old ladies. Give me a shot of tequila. And leave the worm."

The waiter smiled. "Ah, the house specialty! Coming right up!"

As the drinks were being prepared, I shifted nervously in my dainty little tea party chair while a vamping Ruby gazed at me in her loud silence from across the table. Searching for a way to break the tension, I remembered the money and the pictures in my coat pocket. I fumbled them out and onto my lap, then handed them to her, knocking over the centerpiece and burning my hand on the flaming candle as I did.

"Uh, I guess this is what you came for."

Ruby peeked at the pictures for a moment and quickly thumb counted the money. She smiled a satisfied smile.

"Amazing. Simply amazing. Tell me, just how did you manage to do it? The money and everything. McCreedy's a rough customer."

"Oh, there wasn't much to it, really. In fact, it was kinda like takin' candy from a baby. A burly, fish-smellin' tobacco chewin', six foot-four, two hundred and fifty-pound, money crazed baby."

Ruby giggled. But not a silly schoolgirl giggle. It was provocative. Everything she did was provocative. Especially the way she drank. The waiter made our drinks and placed them on the table. Beside Ruby's tequila shot with the fish bait float, the waiter set a bowl of freshly cut limes and a colossal shaker of salt that I figured Lot's wife couldn't have filled.

Ruby shook the salt in a slow circular motion and filled the pocket between the thumb and forefinger of her hand. She licked the salt, picked up the shot with one hand and a lime with the other and tossed back the tequila. Worm and all. The lime followed as she sucked long and hard until all the juice was gone, putting the shriveled peel in the empty glass. Then with a wicked grin, she wiggled the worm between her teeth before swallowing it down like a fettuccini noodle. I was impressed but tried not to show it. Although my drooling might have tipped her off.

Ruby now perked up. "I have an idea. You know, you practically risked your life for me tonight. I think you deserve a bonus. Why don't we go back to my place so I can give it to you?"

"Uh, well, now, ahh, it's not necessary for you to, uh. . ."

Ruby interrupted my schoolboy stuttering by reaching over, grabbing me by the neck and pulling me across the table for a hot, wet, tequila laced kiss that left me with a serious case of localized rigor mortis.

"You wait here. I'm going to the powder room for some more lipstick. You're wearing mine. When I get back, we'll leave. In the meantime, have another drink. You're gonna need it."

Walking away, her hips swung like a hypnotist's watch putting me into a tongue wagging trance. A trance whose power of suggestion was loud and clear until it was broken by a frantic, rattling voice that snapped like a magician's fingers. It belonged to Dusty.

"Webb! Webb! They're back! They've come back!"

I turned and gave Dusty the once over. Once was enough. The aluminum foil that before covered only his hat was now wrapped in one continuous sheet around his entire body and the bent coat hanger had been replaced by an old Rembrandt console antenna with electroplated rabbit ears that stretched out four feet in the air which was stuck to his helmet with gray duct tape that swaddled his head and chin like a mummy's shroud. He was wearing X-ray specs that he had ordered from the back of a Green Lantern comic book and a pair of hip waders tied so tight to his waist, it was a miracle his pants didn't fall down. He was dapper to say the least.

"Is that the way the kids are wearin' em these days?"

"It is if you don't want them Mole Men comin' after you, by God, and they're back! I told you, Webb! I told you their fur lined butts were out there! And now they've come back and tried to get me this time."

"Easy now, Captain Midnight. Just tell me what happened."

"You're damn right I'll tell you! I'll tell you right now! Not more than an hour ago, I was standin' over my sink, mindin' my own business, butterin' a Pop Tart when I looked out my kitchen window and seen 'em! There was four or five of 'em out there with that stream-lined devil machine diggin up that hill! Well, the second I saw 'em, by God I knew what they was doing. They was grave robbin'! I know 'cause I saw the body with my own eyes! They pulled him up like a limp turnip and was gettin' ready to carry him off when I slipped out on the porch with my thirty-ought-six and started blas-tin' and givin' them the banshee scream. "Eat lead Nazi spy Mole Men!" Well, that machine must have had some kind of deflector shield on it like Star Trek cause I didn't get a one of 'em and I'm a shootin' son of a gun! And when them bullets hit that shield, they all jerked around and turned them laser beam eyes at me. I know they tried to suck out my brain! Fortunately, my armor protected me, so I took off runnin' to find you. And here I am. The one who lived to tell the tale. Eye of the tiger. Just like Rambo."

"Rambo. Yeah, that's just what I was thinkin'."

"We've gotta call somebody! The police! The National Guard! The Moose Lodge! Call 'em all! Them Mole Men got to be stopped!"

Dusty ranted and flailed as I patiently endured this manic sideshow. The two thick-necked bouncers were not so patient. They grabbed Dusty from behind and were about to run the jack on him until I stepped in.

"Ho! Hey! Ho! Wait a minute, guys. He's okay. Just a little excited, that's all."

"He's just a little out of his friggin' mind," said one of the muscle twins.

"Don't you know what's goin' on, you big lugghead? There's monsters from the center of the earth comin' to feed off our bones!" Dusty yelled as he threw his arms back, knocking over Ruby's "Land of The Giant's" saltshaker and spilling it on the table. He might as well have broken a mirror while walking under a ladder crossing a black cat's path.

"Oh, Lord, what have I done? Bad luck! Got to reverse the spell!"

Salt went flying as Dusty, now doubly crazed with fear, threw handfuls over both shoulders, most of which hit the bouncers right in the face. With the two meatbags temporarily blinded, Dusty broke away and began running from table to table, grabbing up saltshakers and flinging Morton's best everywhere. Then he grabbed me and filled my pockets full of salt screaming,

"Protect yourself against the evil! Beware! Beware the Ides of Moles!"

By this time the bouncers had regained their sight and clamped down on the frothing fly boy. As they hauled him out, Dusty pleaded and choked as he threw a saltshaker to me. I caught it and slipped it in my pocket as I followed the fracas to the door.

"You've got to stop 'em, Webb! You've got to! You're the only one who can!"

"Stay out of this mister," snapped one of the bouncers, thinking Dusty was referring to them. "Your boy's got to go."

"Just toss him easy, guys," I said, knowing Dusty's brain couldn't stand any further damage. "Don't worry, Ace! I'll be out there tomorrow and we'll save the world from destruction!"

"Remember the Alamo!" cried Dusty as he landed on a nice, soft pile of pavement.

Seeing that Dusty hadn't broken anything important, I turned back toward my table and was met lip to lip by a purring Ruby.

"Let's blow this dump, shall we? My hotel's not far from here and I've got a car waiting, so let's go. I want to see if you really are the last of the full grown men."

I had no time to answer. Ruby slipped a finger inside my belt and pulled me out the door into the back seat of a black limousine. The driver punched it and we screeched off into the grey mist of the city night.

Inside the club, from a secluded tier three table, Wormy had watched the entire scene.

Chapter 9

The Excelsior was a private hotel secluded by a hanging garden courtyard in the middle of the midtown financial district. It had long served as a fortress of solitude and clandestine retreat for the weaselly wealthy that couldn't afford to be seen leaving a seedy no-tell motel. Its muted elegance sharply contrasted the illicit sheet-shaking that took place on its minted pillows. I was reminded of these facts as I did my best face-front elevator stare while riding to Ruby's top floor penthouse, her roaming hands hungrily reading me like a braille menu.

As we entered her darkened suite, Ruby sat me down on a velvet davenport and finally removed her tongue from my ear.

"I have to confess something," she said bashfully. "By now, I'd normally have you stripped down on the floor in a love lock as we writhed a naked passion rumba, but it's just that I'm so shy around you.

You overwhelm me. I mean, the way you handled McCreedy and everything. You're so strong and sure of yourself. I've never, ever met a man like you. And because of that, I want to be good for you. The best. So, you just sit there and relax. I'm going to slip out of this little red number and into something a bit more comfortable. Something I think you'll like. And, when I come back, I want to hold you close and feel your strength. And your passion. I want to feel the pain of your tenderness and know the secrets of your heart. I want our souls to touch in places that before tonight we've been afraid to even know. And then we'll do it!"

Somehow, as I watched her hips twist into the bedroom, she didn't seem so shy.

I was one big sweaty palm as I waited for her. Something more comfortable! I'd heard enough B-movie dialogue to know what that meant, but there had never been anything like Ruby in any movie, anywhere. So I sat, braced and anxious, ready for the big Ta-da. Then, the door opened and there she was. Wearing a black silk V-shaped teddy with a sheer wrap that fell over her shoulders and softly traced the contours of her every curve. She kittened across the floor toward me. I stood and stared, sure that I would never blink again.

Digging the fingers of her left hand into my chest, Ruby curled around behind me and went back to work on my ear. Her right hand began to loosen my tie while the left continued frisking me like an overzealous meter maid. If she was checking for weapons, she was about to find one. As she continued her dexterous assault, I started to relax and enjoy the ride. Two magic hands doing that voodoo, that they do so well. But when I felt a third hand, I knew something was wrong. Real wrong. Unless Ruby had suddenly turned into some kind of mutated circus freak, there was someone else in the room. Someone that was standing right behind me. Someone with very poor hygiene. I turned my head slowly to see a clawed hand from Cleveland tightening its grip on my right shoulder. I froze like a mannequin while my mind raced. Dusty's story. The mound. The worm ranch. Murdock. McCreedy. And Ruby. They were all connected in some way, and as I turned my head, I found out how. Dusty had been right. In the split second before that gloved fist sent me off to dreamland, I knew that crazy hayseed had been right. Standing behind me with glowing eyes, clawed hands and brown slimy skin, were three Mole Men.

Chapter 10

When the alarm went off, still in that waking twilight, I thought my dream had been unusually real. One of those dreams you have to shake out of, and even then, it still hangs with you for a while. This definitely was one of those. Or so I thought. When I tried to get up and shut off the alarm, I realized that the ringing wasn't coming from a clock. It was in my head and with it, the painful pounding of a Gene Krupa bass drum.

I raised myself up as much as I could. The throbbing pain had squinted my eyes as I tried to survey the surroundings of what appeared to be a small storeroom. I could make out a few barrels and boxes in the light that came through the broken pane of glass of a painted window. It definitely wasn't home. I looked out the jagged hole in the window and saw blurred images moving busily inside a large warehouse. As my vision started to clear, I could make out a group of men wearing bulky brown overalls, slick caps and lights attached to their heads. They were digging in huge tanks of dirt and pulling up worms with Stevedore gloves. Gloves that had long, silver claws just like the one I found on Dusty's mound. Just like the old man's in the gift shop. Just like the one that put me to sleep last night. These weren't Mole Men. They only looked like them. These were Worm Men.

Even through the pounding haze in my brain, it all made sense now. Everything came together at once and hit me like a mail train. Unfortunately, so did the gloved fist of the worm worker cum Mole Man whose pre-punch salutation sounded like bad Bogart. It also sounded familiar.

"Sleeping beauty decided to wake up, huh? Back to Wonderland, Alice"

"Alice?" I thought right before the Suzie-Q sent me flying back into the arms of Morpheus. The voice was definitely familiar. So was the punch. Lights out.

Chapter 11

There's only one thing worse than waking up with a piercing headache from a fist induced sleep and finding yourself suspended ten feet in the air swinging on a two chain wench above a huge tank of oozing bilge, and that's doing it to the sound of "Glow Worm" on the saxophone. That's what I heard as I shook myself to. I was hoping it was a remnant of some hellish nightmare, but as I opened my eyes, I saw that I was living it. Live and in person. For below me, in the middle of a steamy, Orwellian bait factory, an audience of worm wranglers was digging the slimy sounds of that slithering sultan of squirm, Wormy Worsham. It was quite a show.

Seeing that his prize had awakened, Wormy hit one last sour note and looked up at his dangling catch.

"Well, it looks like we've hooked ourselves a big one," laughed Wormy with a chorus of sycophantic serfs joining in. He walked over to the tank and called up to me.

"Don't you know curiosity killed the cat, Mr. Wilder? And you are one cool cat, aren't you? If only you hadn't listened to that simpleton. 'Go from the presence of a foolish man, when thou perceivest not in him the lips of knowledge.' Proverbs. Chapter Fourteen. Verse Seven. You should have spent more time in Sunday school, Mr. Wilder."

"Okay, Reverend Fish Bait, can the Billy Sunday rap. I want to know what the hell's going on."

"If you'll please refrain from your use of profanity, I will detail the events that have led up to your present predicament. You see, Mr. Wilder, I am the epitome of excellence in the field of vermicular husbandry. No one else even comes close. My precious babies are known the world over as the Rolls Royce of red worms. And it's all because of divine providence. Mother Nature has seen fit to stain this land with a magical, nurturing potion that feeds my little ones with the sweet milk of her cherished bosom. I call it Vermillite and it only exists here. In my kingdom. And I protect it and my children from those who would seek to do them harm. Like that corruptible swine Murdock. Purely by accident, he discovered its power and sought to use it for his own personal gain. He came here and foolishly tried to persuade me to sell this land. His greed sickened me. He had no respect nor appreciation for this hallowed ground and, when I refused to accept his covetous proposal, he threatened to drill in from an adjacent farm and drain all of the Vermillite, all of that precious elixir, right out from under the ranch and out of the mouths of my innocent children. My babies. Well, I decided that if he was that determined to get the land, maybe I should oblige him. So I planted him in it."

"That's what Dusty saw in his field that night. You and your little henchmen preforming a premature burial with that mystic power drill. No wonder he flipped out."

"Yes. And how unfortunate for you that he did. If he hadn't been sputtering around in that broken-down rust bucket, he would have never seen a thing. He would have never called you and you wouldn't have come out here sticking your nose in where it didn't belong. And consequently, you wouldn't be hanging there like a big mouth bass."

"So the fry cook tipped you off, huh?"

"Dear Thelma did call my attention to your inter-loping, but I had other allies as well. If you'll look down to your left, I'd like to introduce you to one of them."

I looked over to see a worm worker dressed in full digging regalia, his hand on the lever of the chain winch that suspended me above the tank.

"Captain, if you will," said Wormy, and at his request, the worker reached up with his clawed hand and pulled off his mask. It was McCreedy.

"I believe you two have met?"

"Hey there, four eyes. How's the head feel?" McCreedy smiled at me with a green-tooth grin. "It felt pretty good to me when I was punching it."

"It would feel a whole lot better if I didn't have to smell your stench, fish monger," I sneered. "That bath I gave you didn't help much, did it? I'd ask you to hoist me up so I could get away from the stink, but I don't think this thing goes up that high."

"Gentlemen, please. Let's try to maintain a sense of decorum," urged Wormy. "Now, Mr. Wilder as you can see, Mr. McCreedy works for me. And I assume you've figured the rest out for yourself."

"Where is she?"

I had barely finished the question when Ruby walked in. She moved with a slinking smugness as she sidled up next to Wormy and blew me a vain kiss. All of a sudden she didn't look so good anymore. But evidently, she still did to Wormy's henchmen who gawked and grunted at her through their masks. Their crudities incensed Wormy who would not stand for public displays of a carnal nature. He shot them a look that would have made a pit bull flinch.

"Are we keeping you from something?" asked Wormy with a sarcastic ire. The workers needed no further cues from the big boss as they cowered away like druids, leaving Wormy, Ruby and McCreedy to tend to me.

"Forgive them dear. They are not refined."

But Ruby's attention was focused on me. McCready's sucker punch didn't seem to hurt half as much.

"You still want to know the secrets of my heart, Delilah? I'm dying to tell 'em to you now."

"Estarse Quieto, Puerco!"

Her Spanish epithet confused me. Why did this Aryan Amazon suddenly sound like a Mexican dance hall girl? I was about to find out.

"I know what you're thinking, Mr. Wilder," said Wormy, "That she's not the girl you thought she was. And you're right. In more ways than one. Ready for the unveiling, Dulcinea?"

"Si."

With a quick flourish, Ruby pulled off her wig

to reveal a short black pageboy that made her look like she had just stepped out of the chorus line of West Side Story. The last piece of the puzzle had fallen into place. She was the Cuban bombshell. The Havana hussy that sent Murdock over. As I stared sadly toward the floor at Ruby's discarded personality, Wormy introduced me to the new one.

"Allow me to present my personal assistant, Senorita Rubi Caída."

"Ruby Falls. Clever. But not as clever as the way you set up Murdock with those pictures. Tell me, just for grins, how'd you do it?"

"Oh, it was easy. I have a friend at the *Trombone* who's extremely adept at photographic manipulation. It's quite amazing really, the things he can do. For a small fee, of course. You know she and Murdock were never in the same room. But I guess if the price were right, he could put Hitler and Gandhi together and make it look like they were on their honeymoon."

"The next time you see him, ask him to get me an autographed print of that, would you?"

"Consider it done. Except, unfortunately, you won't be around to enjoy it. I'm sure you've been wondering what's in the tank below you."

"It did cross my mind."

"You'll be glad to know that you're going to be devoured by one of the rarest breeds of Brazilian man-eating worms."

"You mean the Spiny-Headed Nematode?"

Wormy was visibly impressed. "Why, yes. Exactly. Are you familiar with this classification?"

"Who isn't? An amphibian worm that evolved from the cross breeding of the South American Piranha and the Equatorial Thunder Slug, that ironically, eats fish. I've heard stories of them picking gator bones clean in under a minute. That's one disagreeable little worm. But, tell me, how are you able to raise a tropical annelid in a temperate zone?"

"Well, that did pose a problem. You see, the first thing I had to do was figure out how to humidify an area large enough to accommodate their breeding method, which, as you know, requires a moist peat for conception coupled with a freshwater birthing pond. So, I designed a two chambered aquarium/terrarium with separate internal temperature gauges. Once that was solved, the question of providing a continuous food supply remained. The difficulty in that was. . . "

Wormy caught himself rambling. So did Ruby and McCreedy who stared at him with perplexed concern. I had hung him up with a classic Three Stooges diversionary tactic and made him look like a buffoon in front of his employees. After an embarrassing slow burn, he cleared his throat and tried to recover.

"Suffice it to say they will get the job done." Wormy curtly regained his composure. "And now, regretfully, I must bid you adieu, Mr. Wilder. In a way, I'm a bit saddened that it had to come to this. You are an interesting fellow. In other circumstances, we might have grown to be acquaintances. Not close, mind you, because of the great chasm between our social classes. But I would have spoken to you if we passed on the street."

"You're just a regular Dale freakin' Carnegie, aren't you?"

"Please don't be bitter. Understand this is not done out of malice but necessity. And, if it eases your mind at all, take comfort in this fact: inevitably, we are all food for the worms."

Then, with cold eyes, he turned to McCreedy and barked, "Drop him!"

I heard McCreedy laugh as he grabbed the lever while Ruby looked on in wicked anticipation. Ruby. She had been in my life for less than twenty-four hours and now she was about to help take it from me. Somewhere along the line I should have figured it out. I should have seen it coming. Somewhere between the office and the club, I should have stopped and. . . the club. The tequila. Dusty. The salt. And the Equatorial Thunder Slugs.

Just as McCreedy was pulling back the lever to release the chain, I quickly reached into my pockets and dumped Dusty's life saving seasoning into the tank. Every neighborhood delinquent performed this cruel trick, I prayed that it would work now. My prayer was answered. Just like slugs on a salty sidewalk, the killer worms began to dissolve. They popped and crackled like frying bacon as McCreedy released the catch dropping me into the tank. As I fell, Wormy, driven by some warped paternal instinct, dove in the pit screaming, "My babies! My babies!" The screaming stopped when he broke my fall. Being a full grown man carries some weight. Literally.

"Nice dive, Louganis. I give it an 8.0. One point off for screaming like a schoolgirl. The other just for tickin' me off."

With Wormy out cold in the tank, I climbed out and was greeted by my Mole Man Moriarty. McCreedy.

"You were lucky the first time, Alice. That was just a little sparring session. This time, it's for keeps."

McCreedy waved the razor-sharp claws of his Stevedore gloves at me like a two-fisted Freddy Krueger.

"Bring your baited breath this way, Popeye, and I'll make you swallow those green teeth!"

McCreedy rushed in slashing with the claws, as I backed away, bobbing and weaving like a Jack-in-the-Box. I kept retreating until I tripped over a crate of imported Peruvian worm dirt and fell hard against a warehouse wall. McCreedy pounced and held the claws in front of my face like a set of leather clad Ginsu knives.

"Time to cut bait, Cowboy," said McCreedy as he drew back and lunged toward me with all ten blades pointing at my face. With split second timing, I ducked as the gloves missed my head and stuck in the wall behind me. Then I rammed my shoulder into McCreedy's chest, knocking him back, leaving the gloves hanging in the wall and McCreedy without his edge. He looked down in disbelief at his bared hands. He shouldn't have. I caught him with a shot to the chops that sent him reeling into a stack of barrels. From then on, it was an old-fashioned Donnybrook with me and McCreedy punching and kicking and smashing up everything in the warehouse while Ruby stood in a corner grabbing bottles of liquid worm feed from a broken crate and firing the bottles at my head. When she finally connected, it wasn't with me, but McCreedy who shook his head and staggered back just far enough to give me room to throw a John Wayne haymaker that landed right on the button. McCreedy went down, with no need for a count. He was out.

"Thanks for the dance, sailor. I'll bring you flowers next time."

As I stood over McCreedy and caught my breath, a screeching Ruby jumped on my back and started pounding a stiletto heel into the back of my head. I whirled around trying to throw her off, but she hung on like a bull rider at the last round-up, until I managed to grab her arm and flip her over my shoulder onto the concrete floor. I thought that would take the fight out of her, but she was one tough Chiquita. She came up from the floor with a two-by-four and swung its bad intentions at me. I sidestepped and caught her arm in mid-stroke, forcing her down on her knees and dropping the board. Her savage grimace quickly melted into a schoolgirl pout as she whined, "Please. Not so hard. You're hurting me. I'm just a girl."

At this point, my chivalry may have been on life support, but it wasn't dead. She was still a woman. That counted for something. So, I let her go and turned to walk away from her. As I turned back for one last look, I saw that it wasn't over yet. Ruby had picked up the plank and was coming toward me with blood in her eyes. That was it. I'd had enough. As she started to swing, I punched her right in her lipstick and put her to sleep.

Then, with an Ernest Tubb flip, I adjusted my hat and walked out of the warehouse and over to Dusty's farm to call the Federalies.

Epilogue

The sign on my office door read "Gone Fishing."
It wasn't a lie. I needed a quiet break and Dusty's
Pond seemed like the perfect place. And it would
have been, if Dusty hadn't come along. He figured I
needed the company. I also needed a pair of ear plugs.

"Yeah, yeah. I told you I saw somethin' out there.
They might not have been Mole Men, but they were
Worm Men and that's pretty close. And they did plant
that feller out there and they were comin' after me. You
gotta admit that."

"Well, the cops have got 'em now and the worm
ranch is shut down, so we don't have to worry about
them anymore."

"Yeah, I guess you're right. Don't have to worry
about them anymore. And that's good 'cause I wanted to
talk to you about somethin'. My dog's been actin' real
strange lately. He's been gnawin' at the furniture like he
ain't been feed in weeks. I swear his bug bitten mind

is bein' controlled by one of those psychotronic machines the Russian secret police were developin'. You know, the one that kept givin' Yeltsin those heart attacks. Either that or Bigfoot's back! I swear I saw a piece of his toenail in my driveway! And every night about dark, my cat starts lickin' his hair agin' the grain. Now that's proof! Here! Look at this toenail! I know you're gonna say that it looks like a piece of an old beer bottle, but I guarantee you it's the genuine article! See? See!"

As Dusty continued his mad ranting, I pulled my hat down over my eyes and thought about Señor Bob's. Tomorrow was "Thirsty Thursday." All the Cérvéza you could drink. I was gonna need it.

The Doll

I t was night on a dark, wet city street in the warehouse district of St. Vegas, Florida. A shadowy figure nervously tried to fit a key into the locked door of a car parked under a streetlamp. His hands were shaking like a hard core drunk with a bad case of D.T.'s when he heard a shot fired in the alley behind him. A flash and two more cracks of the gun were heard as he turned around to see a tall man clutching his chest, stumble out of the alley and stagger straight toward him. He gripped the keyholder's shirt with a bloody hand, gasped and fell to the pavement. A second man carrying a smoking gun came out of the alley and ran to the car.

"What the hell happened?"

"He got wise, so I had to plug him. Now get in the car and let's beat it before the cops get here. Move!"

The two men piled in the sedan and squealed away, leaving the third man lying in the street.

As the car drove out of sight, a plain clothed

police detective ran to the scene, followed by two uniformed officers. The police detective stopped at the
blood-soaked body on the street, leaned over and talked
quietly to it.

"Wilder, I warned you you'd end up like this. I
warned you."

Next
Webb Wilder, Last Of The Full Grown Men
Episode Two "The Doll"

Don't just sit there,
turn this book over
and read "The Doll"

Psychotronic Serenade

I couldn't believe it. I'd already walked five miles and I still hadn't seen one sign of civilization. No people, no houses. No phones, no lights, no motor cars. Not a single luxury. The sun was starting to sink and I didn't want to be stuck out here in the middle of nowhere, trying to find my way back, not being able to see my hand in front of my face. I needed a break. It appeared that the light up ahead just might provide one and it was coming from a phone booth.

Sitting in the middle of a gravel parking lot beside a boarded-up country store, it was one of those old-style stand-up glass booths with an overhead light and a collapsible sliding door. It didn't really matter what style it was, though, as long as the phone worked. I figured if the light was on, it must. I started toward the booth feeling a bit of relief. It was quickly replaced by one that I was being followed. Even though I knew that paranoia was normal in this kind of situation, I was still going to turn around and look just to ease my mind. It wasn't. About twenty yards behind me, stalking me in stride, was a Doberman.

I decided to forget the phone booth and just try to make it to the store. It was closer and would provide better protection if and when the dog attacked. I stepped up onto the porch and reached for the doorknob as he drew closer. The door was nailed shut. I was going to try and force my way in but before I could draw back a shoulder, another Doberman snaked his head around the right side of the store. Now there were two.

I froze when I saw the second dog. I wasn't sure what to do. If I moved, they might leap, if I stayed still, I was a sitting duck. Then, a sharp sound shook an idea into my head. It was a ringing telephone. That was my only option. I'd go for the booth. If I sprinted, I could make it, then I'd call for help. I slowly and carefully started to back off toward the left side of the porch. Both dogs started growling menacingly and I was praying that the ringing phone, which seemed to be getting louder, wouldn't set them off. I had just made it to the edge of the porch and was ready to bolt when I heard something moving above me. I looked up and saw, peering over the edge of the low roof, a third Doberman. Now, I had no choice. I had to make a run for it. My mind raced in a panicked mental conversation. "Don't count down, they'll sense it. Just go. Go as fast as you can. Now!"

I took off and I could hear them coming close behind me. "Move legs, move! A few more steps and we'll make it." I felt one snap at my pants leg as I threw all my weight forward and dove into the booth. I quickly spun around and kicked the door closed, holding it in place with my foot. The dogs went crazy.

They were barking and growling and slamming into the glass in a blood lust frenzy, and all the while, the phone kept ringing louder and louder. It took me a second to get back some of my composure. When I did, I realized that as long as they didn't break through the glass, I was safe. Since the phone was ringing, I thought I'd pick it up and tell whoever was on the end of the other line that I needed help.

"Hello? Hello!"

"Hello there, Wilder. My boys keeping you company?"

"What?!"

"I told you I'd get you, Wilder. I told you. The cops can't hold me. The jails can't hold me. But I'm holding you in the palm of my hand and I'm going to squeeze until your blood runs dry. That's the least I can do for what you did to me. Are you listening, Wilder!"

The voice on the other end belonged to Louie LeCoat. No matter how many times I hung up the phone his maniacal laughter was still coming through the line. I kept my foot pressed tight against the door while the bloodthirsty dogs barked and scratched and pounded on the glass. At this point I hoped I could hold on long enough until someone, anyone would come by and find me. And to make matters worse, I really, really needed to go to the bathroom.

Next
Webb Wilder, Last Of The Full Grown Men
Episode Three "Psychotronic Serenade"

We were easy. Too easy. And they were just mean. I guess I couldn't blame them too much, though. They came by it naturally.

As I watched them hop into a waiting limo, laughing and giggling like a couple of sorority girls during spring break, I couldn't help but think one thing. A blender would have been a lot better gift, after all.

The Doll

a tawdry tale of
assassinations,
psychotic moms and
a little doll
torn in two.

Webb Wilder
Last Of The Full Grown Men

"The Doll"
by Shane Caldwell
& Steve Boyle

Worm Ranchers Publishing LLC

Nashville

Webb Wilder, Last of the Full Grown Men
"Mole Men" & "The Doll"

You're holding a WORM RANCHERS PUBLISHING Mystery Novelette.
Now, wash your hands.

Worm Ranchers Publishing
P.O. Box 58285
Nashville, Tennessee 37205
USA

ISBN: 978-1-7376675-0-6

Library of Congress Control Number: 2021916365

Second Printing 2021
First Edition 1996

for more information visit:
www.WebbWilderLastOfTheFullGrownMen.com
www.WWLOTFGM.com

COVER ART AND GRAPHICS BY
ELVIS WILSON, NASHVILLE, TN

This is book No. 2

If you haven't read "Mole Men," do yourself a favor and turn this book over and start there. If you have read book No. 1, then sit back and enjoy the darker side of every little girl's psyche in "The Doll."

Prologue

Night always falls hard on St. Vegas. It fell hardest on The Boneyard, a burned-out warehouse district on the city's east side, where pony sized roaches battled for turf with hordes of giant sewer rats. Foul and forbidding, it served as a dangerous sanctuary for the thieves and junkies hiding in its black holes. This was the kind of place that made you feel like your own footsteps were sneaking up on you. Like a thousand eyes watched you from the deep darkness. Like you were in the wrong place no matter what the time.

It was almost midnight when an empty bottle of Captain Easy was accidentally kicked out of a narrow alleyway by a skulking figure that splashed across the wet street to a black sedan parked in the dim light of a corroded shell of a streetlamp. With hands shaking like a drunk with D.T.'s, he nervously tried to fit a key into the driver's side door when a shot was fired behind him. There was a flash and two more cracks of the gun were heard as he spun around to see a tall man stumbling out of the alley, clutching his chest and staggering toward him. A bloody hand tore at the shirt of the panicked key holder. He watched dumbfounded as the wounded fish gasped and fell to the pavement. A third man carrying a smoking gun ran from the alley straight to the car.

"What happened? What the hell happened?"

"He got wise, so I had to plug him. I didn't have a choice. Now get in the car and let's beat it out of here before the cops show up. Move!"

The two men jumped in the sedan and squealed away, leaving the third man lying in the street.

As the car drove out of sight, a plainclothes police detective flanked by two uniformed officers, stepped from a warehouse doorway and ran to the scene. They stopped and stared silently at the motionless, blood-soaked body as the detective leaned over and spoke into a still ear.

"I warned you, Wilder. I warned you this would happen."

He then called over his shoulder to the two patrolmen.

"He looks natural, don't he?"

"Yeah, Lieutenant. He makes a real good stiff," laughed one of the cops.

"Too bad he doesn't look that natural when he's pretending to be shot," said the detective standing and nudging the bogus corpse with his scuff-worn wingtips. "Come on, Wilder, get up. Show's over. They're gone."

"What? No curtain call?"

"Curtain call, hell. You're lucky you made it through the first act. I warned you, if you overdid it, it could blow the whole thing. I'm surprised he bought any of it the way you were flailin' around out here. Rasputin didn't take that long to die."

"Really? I thought I brought a refreshing note of subtlety to the role," I said picking myself up and removing my soiled overcoat, "Anyway, he got in the car, didn't he?"

"Yeah, no thanks to you. He probably heard there were a couple of winos doing 'The Mikado' a few blocks over and wanted to drive down and catch it. I hear it's a much better show than the one you put on here tonight."

"You know something, Dombrowski? You're starting to make me feel unappreciated. I mean, I figured out this whole Louie LeCoat thing for you. I set him up, risking my neck doing it. Then, I roll around in this swamp of a street playin' dead just so your boy Hanlon can drive that nutcase off to the Crossbar Hotel while you go back to the station house and run through a gauntlet of backslappers who'll be thinkin' you're the Polish Columbo. And what do I get? A load of wise from you and your two dates there."

"You ought to feel lucky we let you tag along on this one, Sherlock. It'll make a nice little story for you to tell those pathetic lowlifes who are desperate enough to hire you to find their missing kitty-cats. Plus, you're forgetting who approves P.I. licenses in this town. Your participation in this sting tonight might persuade me to look favorably when yours is up for renewal."

"Great. Will it knock a few bucks off your pay-off?"

"That's a filing fee," replied Dombrowski indignantly, "and it's legit."

"Yeah? So's WrestleMania," I shot back as I folded my topcoat over my arm and adjusted the brim of my Resistol, "Well, boys, nice workin' with you. It's been a real slice. In fact, it's been the whole lousy pie. Don't take any wooden donuts. Aloha."

As I turned to walk away, a black and white pulled up beside the lieutenant and his escorts. Mutt and Jeff were piling in the back seat when Dombrowski stopped and called out.

"Hey, Wilder! You want a ride outta here? This ain't no fun park you're walkin' through, you know."

"No, thanks, Festus. It would kill my rep being seen with you. Even down here."

"It's your funeral, tough guy. See you at the morgue," laughed Dombrowski as the police car screeched off into the night, leaving me alone in a maze of crumbling buildings and looming shadows.

Chapter 1

It's all attitude," I reminded myself as I made my way through the darkness of the warehouse war zone, "Just act like you own the place and you can walk barefoot through Hades and not get a blister."

The Boneyard wasn't Hell, but it was pretty close. Most wouldn't walk it on a bet, but I knew that the cowardly vermin burrowed in this stink hole wouldn't take a chance on jumping a full grown man, especially one whose body language had a bad accent. Besides, with the mixed commotion of gunfire and cop cars, the rats had all scurried away and were sweating it out until the coast was clear. The street would be mine. Or so I thought.

About fifty yards ahead, I saw two vague images around a corner moving in my direction. From a distance, they appeared to be on the small side. Maybe a couple of stray Barty Boys, a bunch of pint-sized punks who made up for their diminutive dimensions with sheer numbers. But they never traveled in anything less than double digits and anyway, they were a south side gang that rarely left their own territory. They weren't staggering or swatting at imaginary bats so that ruled out winos and paint huffers. And most of the bums would be curled up in a doorway under a blanket of newspaper by now. These two were hard to figure. Whoever they were, they looked out of place and afraid. When the lights of an oncoming car hit them, I saw why.

They were a young couple, just barely in their twenties, standing wide-eyed and frozen in the high beams. The boy was khakied and buttoned down like he had just stepped out of an L.L. Bean catalog and his pixieish companion's shoulders were draped with Angora and ash blonde curls. Not your typical wrong-side-of-the-tracks residents. More like Hansel and Gretel wandering through a mosh pit. Alone and unguarded, they were primed for danger. The car, which had now hit ramming speed, was about to provide it.

It roared past me, jumped the curb and headed straight toward the boy who had awakened from his Halogen-induced trance just in time to push the girl into the safety of a cracked alcove. But he was still in harm's way as the half ton of wheeled steel bulleted toward him with evil intent. In the blur of action, I focused on the kid who stood in the path of the speeding vehicle like a suicidal matador waiting to be launched into a permanent siesta. Junior looked like a sure goner, but at the last second, he spun away and rolled into the street as the car barely missed running him down. The driver slammed on the brakes and stopped just long enough for me to get a make. It was a dark, two door Chevy Impala with curb feelers and a dealer's tag. Before I could get a read on the red and white plate, he punched it and peeled off down a side alley. All I saw were the last three numbers. 666. Hell on wheels. I hoofed it over to help the fallen youth while the Deathmobile sped away.

The girl and I arrived at the scene together as her gallant young man was unsteadily rising to his feet in a thick cloud of engine exhaust. We both lent a shoulder and carried him over to the trash strewn sidewalk. She had started to cry.

"Oh my God, Colin! Are you all right?"

"Yeah, honey, I'm okay. I just banged up my knee a little. How 'bout you.?"

"I'm fine. Thanks to you."

She wrapped her arms around his neck and began smothering his forehead with lip service after I eased them both down onto the sidewalk. I stepped back and let them have their moment while I tilted my hat back and wiped the excitement off my forehead. After they broke from the clinch, the boy looked up and spoke.

"Can you get us out of here?"

"You mean you've had enough of this captivating scenery?"

"More than enough."

"Yeah, one look'll last a lifetime. You able to motor on that bad wheel?"

"It's okay. We just want to leave."

"We'll be out of here before you know it," I assured my newly acquired charges while helping them to their feet. "I've run this route a few times."

Pressing against me like overzealous bookends, the two frightened waifs followed my lead through the jungle. The piercing quiet of the hollow streets worked on their nerves like a hand-cranked dentist's drill as they imagined back-alley bogeymen jumping out at them from the dark. Seeing Fred and Ginger doing the Paranoid Polka made me think a little small talk might take the edge off.

"Tell me, how'd you two idle youths wind up down here? This place has never been a big draw for the college crowd."

The question startled the boy out of his scared silence.

"Oh, uh, we were coming back from a late dinner at Sir Loin's Pork Palace and I decided it might be nice to take the long way back on River Road and maybe drive down by the pier. I wasn't paying attention and took the wrong exit. Next thing I know, we're in this run-down part of town I've never seen before. And the car dies! I can't figure out what the problem is and there's no one around to help. All the buildings are abandoned and boarded up. There's no phone, no nothing. So, we start walking, thinking we'd get back to the main highway but all we got was more lost and more scared. Then, we heard those gunshots and we both freaked and started running. When we came around the corner, we saw that car. I tried to flag him down but, as you may have noticed, he seemed pretty dead set against taking on any passengers. That's when you came in."

"Sounds like quite an evening. Food, fun and fearing for your life. You don't get that kind of excitement sitting at home watching old reruns of 'Mr. Ed.' Anyway, relax. The real crazies don't come out for a couple of hours yet. You'll be long gone by then."

My "walk-with-me, talk-with-me" schtick had begun to take effect. The more we walked, the more they talked. It was the kind of nervous chatter that comes after a crisis has passed.

"So, are you, like, a homeless person or something?" sniffled the girl while wiping tears from her freshly scrubbed cheek.

Her question raised an insulted eyebrow until I realized my recent dive into the asphalt had left me less than dapper.

"Or something. I'm a private investigator."

"You're a real detective?" asked the boy, "Like Magnum?"

"Yeah, but without the Ferrari. My name's Webb Wilder."

"I'm Colin Crisp and this is my fiancée Daisy Mansfield. We'd like to thank you for coming to help us back there."

"Looked like you didn't need much, Hoss. That was a pretty neat tuck and roll you did after you shoved your intended out of the way. I would've asked for a stunt double."

"Well, I guess you get good at it with practice."

"With practice? You make a habit of playin' chicken without a ride?"

"No, it's just that I've been sort of accident prone lately. In fact, we both have."

"It's true," confirmed Daisy, "That was the second time Colin's almost been run down and last week his brakes failed on his way to pick me up. He had to drive through a hedge in one of the neighbor's yards to stop the car. Poor old Mrs. Leonard. She loved that little dog."

"Daisy's luck hasn't been running much better," added Colin, "Two days ago we were walking in front of the display window at Schwartz's. You know the big one? All of a sudden, the thing just explodes. It was like a bullet hit it or something. Glass was flying everywhere, and a huge section just missed falling on her. It was weird. No explanation for it. And, oh, yeah, tell him about Saturday."

"This was really scary. I was at the racquet club practicing my forehand and the ball machine started going crazy. I noticed at first that it was serving faster than usual, but I thought maybe I had set it wrong or something, so I just kept on returning them. It was kind of fun trying to keep up at first. Then, the balls started coming faster and faster and they started coming harder, too. Real hard. So hard that one of them ripped the strings out of my racket. When that happened, I was like 'Ohmigod!' and just dove on the ground and covered my head. By then, they were coming so fast and hard it sounded like somebody was firing a machine gun over me. When it finally ran out of balls, I got up and saw it had practically shredded the chain link fence behind me. I almost fainted when I saw that. I mean, I could've been killed."

"Sounds like some Hoodoo Witch has put the whammy on you. You two haven't been out to Sadie Rae's place throwin' rocks at her cats, have you? That ol' swamp woman is not one to be messed with."

"No, we haven't done anything like that," answered Colin, "This stuff just started happening a couple of weeks ago. As a matter of fact, it was right after we announced our engagement but that's probably just coincidence, huh?"

"Well, those events do seem to possess a lack of apparent casual connection with your impending nuptials. On the other hand, it could be that somebody's cracked their bat over the fact that you're gettin' hitched. A jealous ex or a psychotic relative, maybe? Can you think of anybody that would fit that bill?"

"Nobody really knows but our parents," said Daisy, "We decided not to tell anyone else until the date was set and everything. We thought we could plan the wedding with a lot less trouble that way. I guess it didn't work, did it?"

"What do Mom and Pop have to say about these close encounters?"

"It's just our moms. Both our dads are dead, and we haven't told either of our mothers about the accidents. We don't want to worry them. They're still having a hard time getting used to the idea that we're getting married. They're kinda freaked about it, you know."

"And hey, maybe tonight was the end of it," said Colin hopefully, "With any luck, we can forget about it and go on."

With any luck. They were definitely due some, but I knew from experience that if you were counting on her, luck was almost never a lady. I also knew that these Perils of Pauline cliffhangers were more than just coincidence. Somebody didn't like the idea of these two saying "I do" and they were going to bizarre lengths to shut them up. They hadn't made good yet, but I knew if they did and I hadn't tried to head them off, I'd be pulling on a bottomless bottle of regret long past last call. So, as we waded through the waist-high weeds on the shoulder of the main highway, I decided to offer my services.

"Listen, you're probably right. It's just been some strange roll of the dice. Your moon's in Jupiter or something. Probably nothing to it but since my professional dance card's not filled at the moment, why don't you let me check into it just to be on the safe side? This way, after I'm done, you can start picking out flatware without having to worry about being attacked by a maniacal tea service. What do you say?"

"I guess it couldn't hurt, could it?" asked Colin.

"I'd feel a lot better," said Daisy, "I think we both would."

"So would I," I said while thumbing the running lights that were topping the hill. "It'll be my wedding present to you. I wouldn't have felt comfortable giving you a blender."

The sound of air brakes proved my opposable digit was still a dependable one as the big semi came to a charitable stop a few yards past our mark. Truckers. Benevolent knights of the open road. Even a pill head doing an eighteen-hundred-mile turnaround could still be counted on for a hitch as long as you weren't wearing jack boots or sporting an "Escaped from Ward C" buzz cut, and these two tenderfoots were one-eighty from that image. As they ran to the open door on the passenger side of the cab, I continued my reassuring rap.

"Tomorrow, I'll go talk to your moms. I won't make a big deal out of it. Just ask a few questions and see if they can point me somewhere. Most likely, in a couple of days, I'll be tellin' you to go ahead and book the preacher."

We made it to the cab as a stubby mitt attached to the fat arm of a pear-shaped Teamster reached down to help Daisy up.

"You folks have car trouble?"

The gearjammer's question reminded Colin that his wounded wheels were still stranded back in the concrete tundra.

"Hey, I forgot! What about my car? Shouldn't we call a tow truck?"

As I helped my naive young friend into the rig, I put on my best mortician's smile and began offering heartfelt sympathies as well as a thorough discourse on the fine art of car stripping while the speedballer put her in low and pulled back onto the highway, leaving the badlands to fade closer than they appeared in the reflection of oversized mirrors.

Chapter 2

Shepherding the lambs through the valley of the shadow had made my late night even later and the morning wasn't cutting me any slack. I squinted in the raw sunlight to read an address scratched on the inside of a matchbook Colin had picked up at Sir Loin's before he and Daisy descended into the maelstrom. The darkness had made it hard to write. So had the thick grease stain that had soaked through the cover. The building number teetered on illegibility, but the street name read like oversized type. Sedgewick Avenue. The St. Vegas Soho District.

Although I knew most of the city like a gypsy cab, this pretentious block of studio lofts, retro coffee houses and makeshift theaters had never been a scheduled stop on the tour. Somehow, sitting in a cluster of Cliff Note Kerouacs swilling lattes while listening to some cadaverous freak dry heaving mental illness and calling it performance art didn't hold much appeal, so I hadn't exactly danced the Cha-Cha when I realized I'd have to visit this beatnik bowery for my chin session with Mom Number One. Fortunately, at this early hour, most of the pasty-faced Daddy-O's were off the streets and in their bunks snoring out clouds of clove cigarette smoke, leaving me to scout for the address with a relative lack of disgust. After a few passes, I found it. The gold placard mounted beside the entrance to the red brick walk-up provided the official verification. The Crisp Gallery of Fine Pop and Kinetic Art. I was about to get culturized.

After opening a heavy mahogany door, I stepped from a small foyer into a reception area decorated with a weird mix of Chesterfieldian elegance and psychedelic chic. A prim young woman wearing a tweed business suit and ankh earrings sat behind an antique desk talking on a princess telephone and scribbling messages with a Bic banana while Peter Max mobiles twisted from the ceiling on either side of her tensile beehive. Around the room were bean bag seats and Day-Glo throw pillows tossed among elaborately upholstered davenports and wing chairs. Burning incense mixed with the smell of fine leather and the diamond glow of a grand chandelier was aided by a collection of multi-colored lava lamps. It was as if the cast of "Hair" had redecorated the lobby of the Algonquin. I eyeballed this hybrid decor as I moved to the desk where Gal Friday was hanging up the phone.

"Effectively eclectic. A marriage of styles that most wouldn't send on a lunch date, but it works. Sort of."

"May I help you?" she asked with detached coolness. No laugh. No smile. No nothing. No need for the pithy P.I. bit, then. This ice dolly was all business.

I figured I'd better get down to mine.

"Webb Wilder. I'm here to see Mrs. Crisp concerning her son. I was told she'd be expecting me."

"Oh, yes. The investigator. I'll let her know that you're here. Please feel free to tour the gallery while you're waiting."

"Don't I need a ticket or something?"

"This isn't a ride, Mr. Wilder. All you need is an open appreciation for the myriad of artistic expressions resulting from the dynamic social and political changes of a tumultuous decade."

"I may have left that in my other coat. But, what the heck? I'll give it a shot anyway."

"To your right," pointed this hipped-up Miss Hathaway, "The exhibits are clearly marked. And please, no fondling."

"Never in public," I smiled as I passed through the arched entrance into the main gallery. Once inside, I saw that the lobby had only been a prelude to more extreme eccentricity. The architecture boasted the refined aestheticism of the Louvre but the objet d'art looked like they had been gleaned from a head shop rummage sale. Red fishnets hung from the ceiling. On the walls, ornate frames worthy of bordering masterpieces held black light posters, old album art and cheesy bachelor pad etchings. Beautifully sculptured columns, each supporting a leopard skin pill box, lined the hallway that led through the tangle of a beaded door into a time warp of Age of Aquarius icons they had dubbed the "Peace, Love and Mary Jane Wing."

Stepping into this strobe-lit room made me feel like I was having a brown acid flashback. In what appeared to be a still life combination of Hullabaloo and

Haight Ashbury, mini skirted mannequins wearing vinyl go-go boots were posed in mid Frug with stiffened partners dressed in Nehru jackets and crushed velvet bell bottoms while replicas of zipper headed flower children assumed the Lotus around a bearded, tie-dyed dummy frozen in a mute rendition of "Kumbaya." Surrounding this counterculture creepshow were walls covered with anti-war graffiti and ascending tiers filled with a Chinese menu of hippie memorabilia. Everything from love beads, water pipes and an original copy of Quotations from Chairman Mao to a nonpareil collection of troll dolls. Accompanying this visual assault was a grating soundtrack of sitar music that would have wigged out the Maharishi. I was still tripping when a sniffish voice provided a welcome shot of verbal Thorazine.

"Quite loathsome, isn't it?"

I turned to see a pinch-faced little man wearing a three-piece Armani that hung from his rail thin frame like a silk toga. He crossed his bony arms and continued his Rex Reed rip.

"To think that a group of scraggly, hallucinogenic hoboes with long hair and dirty feet defined style for an entire generation literally sours my stomach. I detest this exhibit."

"Well, it's not exactly soothing, but neither were the sixties."

"Indeed, Mr. Wilder. Oh, allow me to introduce myself. Norman J. Nance, Ms. Crisp's personal assistant. I was just told of your arrival. If I had known you were here, I could have spared you the discomfort of this psychedelic nausea. Come with me and I'll show you some genuinely intriguing artifacts."

"Groovy," I smirked, raising a mocking

peace sign as I followed his cupped-under walk out of pop art purgatory into an adjoining wing. Watching Pencil Neck jangle in his oversized suit, I bet myself that this pantywaist had sand kicked in his face more than a few times. In the next couple of minutes, I would reconsider my wager.

"While the Crisp Gallery does choose to present certain cultural aspects of the decade that I find utterly repugnant, there is one particular display for which I do possess a great affinity," explained Nance breathing heavy with anticipation as he stopped in front of two doors that looked like they had been carved right out of the Iron Curtain. "The Cold War is most often remembered by the unenlightened proletariat as a frighteningly ominous period in our history. Nuclear proliferation. Assassinations. Espionage. Singing nuns. These were all perceived as sinister and evil. I, however, see them as sublime artistic expressions of man's infinite capacity to subvert and destroy. And behind these doors, Mr. Wilder, you will find a fond tribute to that marvelous virtue. I give you the 'Death, Doom and Destruction Wing.'"

Nance's Strangelove spiel had me doing a blinking double take as he opened the doors with a foppish flourish. I went for the triple when I saw what was inside. An arsenal of weapons that would have made a Ninja drool. Guns, knives, bombs, silencers, cross bows, throwing stars, nunchakus, garroting wires, blow guns and poison darts were skillfully arranged among bona fide versions of John Steed's umbrella, Derek Flint's cigarette lighter, Odd Job's hat and other double-o doodads that went along with a license to kill. The Smithsonian may have had dinosaur bones and Fonzie's jacket, but they didn't have anything like this.

Kind of made me wonder why this place did.

"Expecting trouble?"

"No, no," answered Nance with a sly smile, "but if trouble were to arise, I assure you this room would provide more than the adequate means necessary to quash it. With extreme prejudice."

"Looks ain't deceiving, huh? You know, if you threw in a hundred or so gallons of distilled water and a case of beef jerky, you'd have a survivalist's wet dream. Hey, man alive! You've even got a Six Finger. I had one of those when I was a kid. Little fake plastic job that fit between you're thumb and forefinger. I remember it could shoot a dart, it had an ink pen and there was even a secret compartment behind the third knuckle. Cool toy. I wish I still had mine, but my mother gave it to a church bazaar. Say, who designed this armory for you, anyway? 'Q'?"

"Actually, this is my creation. I am solely responsible for the procurement and presentation of the pieces that are displayed in this wing and as a result, I do possess a bit more than a layman's proficiency in their use. If I may."

As I watched Nance unlock a display case marked "Edged Weapons," I was hoping my glib cracks of wise hadn't peeved him. He may have looked like a weak sister but the way he caressed that blade he pulled out of the case coupled with his fifth column commentary was starting to give me the willies. Sort of the same feeling you'd get attending a taxidermy seminar at the Bates Motel.

"That's some frog sticker you've got there. A bit too fancy for mumblety-peg, I'd say."

"This is a Siberian throwing knife, Mr. Wilder,

circa nineteen sixty-two. Most accurate and deadly. Perfect for the silent kill. Please allow me to demonstrate. If you will just back up against that wall, extend your arms and spread your legs approximately two feet apart."

Wait a minute, now. I'd seen that Ed Ames clip on Carson enough times to know that I didn't want to play William Tell with this little psycho. Even if he had bull's eye aim, I wasn't about to expose my batter to a possible wild pitch. Unfortunately, as I backed off raising my hands in good natured protest, I had pretty much assumed the position.

"No, thanks. I'll take your word for it. Silent and deadly and all that other stuff. Not necessary to show me. I'm a believer, yes sir."

"Stay right where you are and don't move," drooled Nance with a sadistic gleam, "This should be quite a rush."

He was already in his wind up, so I had no choice but to stand still and think thin. With the glint of the blade flashing danger, I closed one eye and watched my life pass before me as he let fly. I was just finishing the eighth grade when the film was stopped by the sound of breaking glass. The hilt of the knife had smashed a cabinet door that was about ten feet away from me. It appeared Nance's slight miscalculation had kept me from harm. That and the fact that he threw like a girl. The bet was back on.

"Wait! Wait! That was just practice! I'll do it this time!"

I bit back an ear-to-ear watching Normie scramble to find his lost toy. While he was searching for his, however, I decided to reclaim one of mine. I grabbed that Six Finger off the shelf and slipped it in my pocket. Hey, it could have been the same one. Who knows? And besides, I was tired of getting along with just five.

Although I wasn't feeling any guilt for lifting the finger, I was starting to feel kind of sorry for Nance. He was a pretty pitiful sight crawling around on the floor begging for a do-over so I was glad when a sharp-edged shout brought him to his feet. It saved him from further humiliation. It also helped cover my snickering.

"Norman! I have told you repeatedly that this sort of rowdy-dow will not be tolerated! This is an art exhibit not a circus sideshow! Now go and fetch a broom to tidy this mess."

"Certainly, Ms. Crisp! Terribly sorry! I was just giving Mr. Wilder a demonstration. Won't happen again. Absolutely not. Never again. Well, I'm off."

The little toady blazed an obsequious trail out of the room as the beneficiary of his boot licking made her way toward me with an outstretched hand.

"How do you do, Mr. Wilder? I'm Felicity Crisp. Colin's mother," she said with more than a trace of a British accent, "Please forgive my hyperactive assistant. He becomes a bit overexcited when he spends more than a few seconds in this wing. Just can't seem to control himself."

"Maybe he should try thinking about baseball. I hear it works for some guys."

"I'll pass that along. Let's move to my office, shall we? It's more conducive to conversation. No flying cutlery to disturb us there."

"After you, ma'am."

She hung a louie out of Nance's playhouse and headed down the hallway at a fast clip. I had to double time it to catch up but it gave me a chance to give her a quick once over from her blind side. Trimmed in a black Edwardian jacket and capped by long straight strawberry blonde hair that must have been ironed flat, Colin's mater was distinctively stylish in elegant 60's Carnaby Street chic. Nice caboose, too. As she moved with a purpose toward her office, Felicity Crisp looked like the name implied. Sounded like it, as well.

"In addition to Norman's antics, allow me to apologize for my tardiness. I was meeting with two gentlemen who wished to purchase some of the gallery's pieces for a proposed themed restaurant chain. Their concept centers around filling their dining establishments with outrageous memorabilia in order to create some sort of absurd theme. Have you ever heard of anything so bloody ridiculous?"

"Sounds like a lead balloon to me."

"I declined their offer, of course. I do have my reputation to protect as well as the gallery's. And Colin's. Ah, here we are. Come in, please."

As she invited me into her office, I got set for another flurry of flower power to bust me in the chops. I thought if she was the one responsible for the museum's bizarro look, then her private digs would have to lean toward the flippy. Once inside, I was forced to think again. It looked like any other executive inner sanctum with dark wood, indirect lighting and a couple of high back chairs angled in front of an oversized desk. Pretty standard stuff. Except for one thing. In a corner, to the right of her desk, was a shrine that would have made The Buddha jealous. A blanket of white lilies and red roses cascaded an extensively detailed frame resting on a large marble pedestal that was lit up like a film premiere at Grauman's Chinese. Inside the frame, posed in profile and glimmering in the crossfire of the spotlights, was that American Ideal of Womanly Beauty and Flawless Feminine Form. The Everlasting Image of Unobtainable Physical Perfection. The Plastic Goddess herself. Barbie.

This wasn't any regular old Barbie, though. Something about the way she stood wearing a pink two piece A-line with matching handbag and pill box hat gave her a strange surrealism. Strange but familiar. I probably should have strode down to the nitty but I couldn't let conversation bait like this float by without at least a nibble.

"Let me guess. Christmas Sixty-four. You got this, a pony and a Mystery Date game."

What I thought was a harmless little icebreaker stopped Ms. Crisp cold. She sat staring at the deified dolly like she had time tunneled back to some painful childhood memory that still hurt when she put too much weight on it. I sat there with innocent guilt smeared on my face hoping she'd snap out of it before I had to taste much more shoe leather. When she did, she picked up on it like she'd never left.

"Not exactly, Mr. Wilder, but it is a rather prized possession. That's an original 'First Lady' model, designed in the summer of nineteen sixty-three and scheduled for release in December of that same year. Of course, due to obvious circumstances, it wasn't. They felt it would be in extremely poor taste to distribute a doll that might be perceived as mocking a national tragedy and in order to insure there would be no chance of that happening, all of them were destroyed. All except this one."

"The one that got away. Must be pretty valuable."

"Quite, but her value to me is not merely mone-tary. It's what she symbolizes. While other cultural icons fade from view, fall out of fashion or simply die, Barbie endures. She adapts. She survives. These are qualities to which I have aspired since assuming the responsibility of managing the gallery from my late husband. It has not been an easy task. Not so long ago, the Crisp Gallery was seen as a stuffy old museum filled with meaningless relics and boring works of art that attracted little interest and much dust. Mostly, it served as a storehouse for the worthless baubles and trinkets that Colonel Crisp col-lected during his numerous travels abroad. Wretched portraits done in paint-by-numbers style by starving street artists, and crude pieces of pottery molded out of elephant dung by toothless aborigines, did not serve to increase the gallery's popularity. But my husband was a stubborn man and he refused to listen to my ideas for renovation and modernization. 'We must maintain our integrity' he would always say. Well, jolly good, but while he was busy maintaining integrity, we continued to lose money and face. It was most humiliating. So, after his rather untimely death, I set about to turn this gallery into a unique and thriving repository of art and culture from what I considered to be one of the most exciting, diverse and socially significant periods in recent history. It was through the same perseverance represented by this doll that I was able to accomplish just that."

"Yeah, you probably wouldn't have received that kind of inspiration from Midge. Anyway, you've really done something with the place. It's definitely unique. And you did it all by your lonesome, too. Tell me, when did your husband pass away?"

"Almost four years ago. It was quite tragic, actually. He and Norman were on one of his countless expeditions to Africa to bring back more of those hideous tribal masks when they were attacked by a tribe of renegade pygmies. Colonel Crisp was felled by a poison dart but Norman somehow managed to elude them and when he returned with the authorities, there was no sign of my husband or the pygmies anywhere. Little devils probably cooked and ate him. The bastards."

"There's an advertisement for vacationing at home. Sorry. I didn't mean to call up a painful memory."

"Think nothing of it. It's long past. Let's proceed to matters at hand. Namely, your concerns about my son. He told me this morning that there have been some recent chance occurrences which you feel may be more than mere happenstance. That someone may be intent upon doing him harm. Is that correct?"

"You are correct, ma'am. Both he and his fiancée have been rattling danger's doorknob lately and given that these 'occurrences' started just a few days after they were engaged, I'm not so sure that you can tag them as chance."

"Do you have children, Mr. Wilder?"

"Nope."

I spared her the "none that I know of" line. I'm sure she appreciated it.

"Well, as a parent, let me inform you of a simple fact of life. Children have accidents. It's all part of growing up. When they are small, their accidents tend to be small. A skinned knee, a bloody nose and the like. Subsequently, as they grow, their mishaps tend to increase in kind and, while she may find it difficult, a mother must eventually step back and let her child make his own way. Use his own judgment. Even when it is woefully poor as, say, in his choice of a mate."

"I take it you don't approve of the possibility of Daisy callin' you Mom someday."

"I don't approve of her in any way, shape or form. No sort of accident could bring him greater harm than going through with his dreadful plan to marry that horrid little girl."

Her curt response coupled with that squinting tic in her left eye led me to believe that she and Daisy wouldn't be getting together for a spot of tea anytime soon. The subject of young Miss Mansfield was definitely a sore one. I decided to poke at it a little and see if something might ooze out.

"You know, I met Daisy last night and she seemed like a nice kid to me."

"Don't be fooled by that Pollyanna veneer. She's ill-mannered and ill-bred. Of course, I suppose one can't place the blame entirely on her empty little head. It is obvious that she was raised, not reared. And that is the fault of her less than savory family. They are a vulgar lot."

"Does Colin know how you feel?"

"He knows that if he marries, it will be against my wishes and without my blessing. What he doesn't realize is that I have worked tirelessly to restore and protect our family's reputation and bringing that tatty tart into our midst could do irreparable damage to us all. As of yet, I haven't been able to convince him of this but as I told you earlier, sometimes, all a mother can do is sit back and hope for the best. In this case, that task has become Herculean."

"A regular Augean stable of emotional

road apples. Well, look, I didn't come by to stir anything up. I just wanted to let you know that your son has had some close shaves recently and maybe someone ought to try and make sure he doesn't get nicked."

"Really, Mr. Wilder, it's not at all necessary. These are strange coincidences. Nothing more. However, I am aware that you and Colin have made some sort of arrangement. If it serves to allay his fears, then far be it from me to stand in the way. I only ask that you please be discreet."

"Don't worry. I'll be the better part of valor in a plain brown wrapper," I assured as I stood to leave, "Nice seeing you, Ms. Crisp and ditto for your gallery. Contrary to what your receptionist says, it is quite a ride. A little bumpy here and there but I'd go again."

"Thank you," she said showing me the door, "And thank you for your concern for my son. It is appreciated but as I told you, there's no reason to worry. No harm will come to my Colin. I'm certain of that. And I'm sure you have more important affairs that require your attention."

"Yeah. There's the one with the mayor's wife and her podiatrist but I'm still waiting for the film to be developed on that, so right now I'm free to give Colin's case top billing."

"How fortunate. He'll be so pleased. Good day, Mr. Wilder."

She smiled goodbye but her eyes didn't join in. As I nodded my adios, I caught one last shot of Camelot Barbie before the shutting door punctuated a curious feeling that had been growing ever since I set foot in the joint. Maybe it was the schizo decor that gave it to me. Or that weasely Nance and his weapons fetish.

Maybe it was the way Ms. Crisp seemed more con-
cerned about her family's rep than her son's health or
that she wasn't exactly thrilled I was on the case. Or
maybe it was that pink Dealey Plaza dress that doll was
wearing. Could have been any of those things, but most
likely it was knowing that I still had my rendezvous with
Daisy's mom waiting for me. From the address, it
looked to be about a three beer ride out to her place. If it
was anything like this spook house, I was gonna need
'em.

Chapter 3

I decided to forgo the liquid reinforcements before meeting Momma Mansfield. It wouldn't be professional to greet a client with booze on my breath at this early hour. Besides, I stopped at seven Gas 'N Go's and none of them carried Mickey's, so with my brand loyalty intact, I entered the soulless confines of suburbia sans blinders.

As I drove past the clusters of cookie cutter ranch houses, I imagined hordes of overworked, gray flannel dads returning home from the office each day to trip over ottomans and be greeted with a sanitized peck on the cheek by their Junior League spouses and their two point-five children who've been waiting in cheery anticipation for the Old Man to doff his tie, don his apron and fire up the backyard grill while Mom serves lemonade and plays cheerleader for the participants in a highly contested family badminton tournament as the smoky lure of barbecue and burgers brings cloned legions of Bermuda-shorted neighbors skipping across manicured fescue bearing bowls of potato salad and morbidly boring tales of lawn mower maintenance to further enhance the pageantry of this middle class suburban sacrament. Ain't that America. No wonder some of these guys snap.

I passed through this nightmare of conformity relatively unscathed to find myself teetering on the edge of Glen Meade, a narrow, secluded valley that corralled herds of hoity-toitys behind a stone barricade that completely encircled the area. Obviously, the Brahmans who occupied this lush little dell didn't want members of any lower castes fouling these pristine surroundings with their leprous presence. As I pulled the coupe up to the security gate, I thought I might fit that bill. The hammer headed security guard who lumbered out of the gate house thought so, too.

"This is a private drive. Authorized vehicles only."

"It's Simonized. Does that qualify? You know, it's amazing what that stuff can do for a car's finish. Just look at that shine."

"Tell you what, Cowboy. I'll look at it while you're turning this heap around and moving it outta here."

Normally, them's fightin' words when somebody insults Trigger, but I could tell that Baby Huey was having a bad morning and it was easy to see why. Sitting in a coffin-sized sweat box eight hours a day being sniffed at by a passing parade of stiff-necked snobs probably wouldn't have me in the running for Mr. Congeniality either, so I decided to can the wise guy routine and let him slide. Hopefully, he'd return the favor.

"Hey, Chief, I wasn't trying to pull your chain. Just making conversation, that's all. My name's Wilder. I've got an appointment with one of your residents. A Ms. Lacey Mansfield."

He leaned back with the wary look of a bartender checking I.D.'s on prom night before plodding off to check my story. After consulting the guest list, he reluctantly buzzed open the iron gate that sealed off the entrance to this suburban Shangri-La and waved me through with all the cordiality of a road crew flagman. Nice meeting you, too, Tiny.

Leaving Rent-a-Cop in his outhouse, I headed down a winding lane past dozens of stately pleasure domes that sat on picture-perfect lawns bordered by rows of sedate palms. I stood out like a Clampett as I tooled along this posh parkway checking for the address while checking out the scenery. Most of these old cribs were so swank they would have given Gatsby mansion envy. Even if this trip turned up nada, it would still be a kick to take a stroll through one of them. Any of them. Except the one just ahead on the left. In the middle of all these palatial estates, what looked like a combination of Late German Gothic and Early Mike Brady jutted out from its hillside perch like a stucco gargoyle. A slanted roof covering a wedge of mirrored glass joined the base of a medieval tower which was buttressed by a bi-level wing that held all the charm of a pump station at a sewage treatment plant. This thing looked like a nightmare Frank Lloyd Wright had after eating bad clams. And to top it all off, they had painted the mother pink. Man, if it looked this bad on the outside, I'd sure hate to see what it looked like on the inside. Unfortunately, I was going to have to. The minnow-shaped nameplate hanging from the beak of the plastic flamingo roosting at the end of the drive read Mansfield. Of course!

I was none too thrilled about visiting this post-modern monstrosity but as I pulled up to the front entrance, I had at least one thing going for me. Unlike the gallery, this place let you know what you were in for right up front. No matter what was waiting for me inside these Pepto Bismol walls, I figured I'd be braced for it. Of course, my figures had been wrong before. I had Liston over Clay in three, the Orioles in sixty-nine and Colonel Mustard in the drawing room with the lead pipe in the championship round of the Clue Invitational at Detection Connection. Wasn't even close. With that in mind, I cinched up a couple of extra notches before I rang the bell and waited for Lurch to answer the door. He never showed. Nobody did. After a while, I thought about enforcing the five-minute rule and making tracks but that would've just meant a return visit out here to Crackerbox Palace and that idea was not an appealing one. Neither was the idea of letting Daisy down. She seemed pretty worried about the accidents. Worried, upset and just plain scared. She had cried most of the way home and the memory of those tears rolling down that sweet little mug made me even more determined to see this thing through. Whoever this bully was, he wasn't going to take her milk money anymore. I was going to make sure of that.

I decided to wander around the grounds while I waited for the lady of the house of horrors to return. Since there weren't any electric fences or "Beware of Dog" signs, I assumed it would be a relatively safe hike. And it was, right up until I saw the fountain. It was a big, freaky-looking sculpture that sat in the middle of a garden full of weeds and dead flowers, showing a fat, naked dwarf perched on a turtle's back holding a harpoon in one hand and his overflowing willie in the other, while a concrete vulture engaged in mortal combat with a cobra that was coiled on top of the shell jockey's head like a fanged turban. Here was an image that was going to haunt me for a while. But, despite the fact that this sickening effigy was so revolting it could have been used to induce vomiting at a poison control center, I couldn't stop looking at it. It was like staring at the head of Medusa except I don't think that old Gorgon broad would've left me half this stoned. I was uncomfortably numb. Hypnotized. I was even starting to hear music. Psychedelic music. It wasn't coming from the fountain, though. Not unless Miguelito the Turtle Boy could thump out "In-A-Gadda-Da-Vida" on that whale sticker of his. As I listened, it sounded like it was coming from the other side of an overgrown hedge that enclosed the back lawn like a horseshoe fence. Maybe there was someone in there that could give me some info on Ms. Mansfield's whereabouts but looking around at this shaggy shrubbery, there didn't seem to be a gateway or archway or any way inside. None, that is, except just plowing my way through. I might get a few scratches and scrapes, but it would be worth it if it moved this case along. It would also get me away from the fountain. That little dwarf was starting to give me the creeps.

I emerged from the bushes without a mark. A testament to my skills as a contortionist as well as the durability of sharkskin. Brushing away the leaves and twigs that had hitched a ride on my rig, I zeroed in on the source of tunes. They were coming from an old stereo Hi-Fi loaded with a stack of 45's and resting on a metal TV cart that sat next to a redwood deck chair. The chair, with its back to me, was close enough to the edge of a kidney shaped swimming pool that its occupant was making circles in the water with lavender toenails. Could be this was Ms. Mansfield. Or a goldbricking maid. Or a weird pool boy. Whoever it was, the fact that they were poolside explained why they hadn't answered the door. However, it wouldn't keep them from answering a few questions. I approached from the rear but fanned out wide so my sudden presence wouldn't surprise them. Little did I know, as I came around to the front of the lounger, I was the one in for a surprise.

"Excuse me. My name's Webb. . . Whoa!"

I quickly turned my head and pulled the brim of my hat down over my eyes. It's the only polite thing to do when one sneaks up on a completely naked lady.

"Webb Whoa? Oh, yeah. The private fuzz Daisy was telling me about. I thought your name was Wildman or something."

"It's, uh... it's Wilder, ma'am and I'm... really... I'm very, very sorry... really."

"What for, man? It's cool. Daisy hipped me that you'd be comin' by to rap about all this bad Karma that's been comin' down on her. I was just soakin' up some rays until you got here, man."

Fuzz? Bad Karma? Overuse of the word "man"? I hadn't heard this much counterculture slang since the last time "Billy Jack" played on the late show. And the thing was, she sounded for real. That would explain why she hadn't flipped out when I caught her with her chassis exposed. Your peaceniks weren't known for having an overabundance of inhibitions and it appeared this one had eighty-sixed hers a while ago. I still had a few of mine left, so I kept the safety on my hat locked in the "on" position while we spoke.

"So. . . I'm guessing you're Daisy's mom?"

"I'm not her mom, man. Not at all. Oh, I gave birth to her and nurtured her and everything but I'm not her mom. And she's not my daughter. We're not into labels, man. I'm Lacey and she's Daisy. We relate to each other as equals, as individuals, as people. No phony role-playing or any of that jive. We are who we are, you know?"

A simple "yes" would have sufficed.

"Well, hey, that's. . . that's very. . . you know. . . with it. Anyway, I wanted to come by and talk. . . I mean, rap. . . about some of these. . . uh, heavy. . . heavy scenes that have been uh. . . hassling Daisy lately."

"You look uptight, man. You must be bakin' out here in those threads. Let's go hang out inside where it's cool. I'm out of cocoa butter anyway."

Seeing her feet hit the ground and start toward the house, I followed close behind, still tugging on my brim, although not as tightly as before. I was a lot less self-conscious now that I didn't have quite as many eyes staring back at me. Besides, as an investigator, it was my job to observe and what I observed was that, evidently, eating sprouts and tofu did a body good. It sure had for Lacey Mansfield. As I slowly tilted up to get a better shot, I could see that, in her day, this chick had probably been pretty popular around the commune. I could also see me getting busted in mid ogle if I wasn't careful. Not that she'd mind me looking but I didn't want her to get the idea that I was some kind of leering pervert who spent his afternoons buying table dances down at The Strip Mall, especially since I'd come there to talk about Daisy. That kind of image didn't usually instill confidence in a client, no matter how much free-thinking cosmic crapola they spouted. I thought maybe some conversation might help the situation. At least it would keep me from staring. I knew I couldn't talk and view butt at the same time.

"I want to apologize again for just walking up on you like that. I rang your bell, but I guess your help didn't hear."

"My help? Are you puttin' me on?" she said, shooting me a hard look over a soft shoulder. "That is such a totalitarian concept. There's no way I'd have anything to do with that kind of fascist oppression. Besides, who needs servants when I've got Frank? Frank takes care of everything."

"Frank. Is he your. . . ?"

"Frank's Frank, man."

"Well, I appreciate your frankness. I was doing that labeling thing again, wasn't I? Sorry. I guess I wasn't thinking. I'm embarrassed about it. . . quite frankly."

That sparkling bit of repartee mercifully came to an end as we stepped through a ritzy revolving door that gave me the feeling I was about to walk into the Plaza Hotel. It was a feeling that passed quickly. I found myself in the middle of a space age bachelor's den that made the Jungle Room at Graceland look subdued. A big, black, low-riding, leatherette boat of a couch floated on a sea of orange shag across from a couple of chairs that looked like they'd been picked up at a Jetson's garage sale. A cheesy rumpus room bar complete with padded stools and a set of monogrammed hi-balls stretched out toward a white brick fireplace accented with a bear skin rug that would have made a comfy little cot for Hef and his pipe. There were rubber tree plants in every corner and pleated leopard skin covered the walls all the way from the floor to the mirrored ceiling. If the King had seen this place he would've turned to Sonny and Red and said, "Now, that's tacky, man." I was still choking back my reaction when my bare lady offered some hip hospitality.

"Hang here a minute, Stretch, while I go throw something on. I'll only be a sec. The bar's over there. Make yourself comfortable."

"I'll do my best," I said as I watched her bounce down the hall.

Left alone in this overblown replica of Matt Helm's living room, I felt about as comfortable as a newlywed husband standing in the middle of the lingerie department on his first shopping trip with the wife. I was looking hard for a spot that provided the least amount of visual abuse when my sinuses were hit with a putrid mix of musk oil and Martinizing fluid. It was a stench so strong you could taste it. The smell knocked my head back and I saw, in the ceiling's reflection, a loud, hairy blob of polyester standing behind me. Great. Here was another weird agent for me to deal with. At least this one was wearing clothes.

I turned to meet a fat but familiar face, one I couldn't place right away. A bushy stache spreading out over a suspicious frown matched the long, stringy hair that hung down past the collar of a madras sport coat from the Johnny Carson Collection featured in the men's fashion section of the nineteen seventy-three

Sears Spring and Summer catalog. The jacket was ill-fitted over a pink shirt, unbuttoned to reveal a thick gut and a gold medallion that rested on a sweaty mat of salt and pepper chest hair while a wide, white belt desperately tried to hold up a pair of lime green golf slacks. He definitely had the style. I tried to ignore it as I responded to his curt questions

"Who the hell are you?"

"I the hell am Webb Wilder."

"What the hell are you doing here?"

"I'm here to speak to Ms. Mansfield."

"Where the hell is she?"

I was about ready to tell this guy to *go* to Hell when I remembered where I had seen him before.

"Hey, aren't on TV?   The car commercials, right?"

"Well, yeah, I do a couple of those," he said relaxing the frown a bit.

"I knew it! You're him! The guy in the strait jacket! You're Krazy Kilgore!"

The frown turned into a proud, beaming smile.
"Of Kilgore's Klassic Kars. At your service! Say, is that your '55 Bel Air out front?"

"Yep. That's mine."

"She's a beauty. A real classic. I'm driving a '65 Goat myself. Got a three eighty-nine bent eight with triple deuce carbs. It'll dust a Vette in the quarter. Before this, I was in a '64 Chevy. The week before, it was a '59 T-Bird. That's the cool thing about owning a dealership, especially one like mine. I can drive a different car every day if I want. Just depends on how I feel. One day, it might be a muscle car. The next, a limo. I got 'em all. You should come by and see me. I'll fix you up with a real sweet deal."

"I might take you up on that sometime. Of course, I bet you've got tons of people coming by with all those wild spots you do."

"Yeah, they work pretty good, man. I write them myself, you know."

"No way! Really? They're something else!"

Yeah. Something else that made you want to throw a brick through the screen. A demented, morbidly obese car hustler bound with leather straps screaming his outrageous prices so close to the camera you could count his fillings. They were the most obnoxious commercials since that old lady fell and couldn't get up, and right in front of me was the jerk responsible for them. I didn't know what he was doing here but since I had him hooked on my line of bull, I figured I'd play with him a little before I threw him back.

"This may seem like a strange request but, could you do some of your act for me? I mean, if you don't mind. I really get a kick out of those things."

"Gee, I don't know if. . . "

"Oh, come on. Do it. Pleeeze."

"Well, okay. Anything for a potential customer!"

Setting himself like a sumo wrestler, KK simulated state-approved restraint by wrapping his pudgy arms around his huge belly and thrashing like a rabid walrus as he began his imbecilic rant.

"Crazy? Am I crazy? You'd better believe I am! I'd have to be out of my mind to offer you insane deals like these! I'm talking low-low-lobotamy prices! So check yourself in to the auto asylum down at Krazy Kilgore's Klassic Kars where we're committed to giving you the craziest deals in town."

What a sap. What a maroon. What a pathetic display. I thought it would be fun seeing him make a complete fool out of himself, but I just wound up feeling embarrassed for the guy. It turned into pity when Lacey entered the room.

"Frank! Can that commercial crud, will you? It really harshes my vibe. It's bad enough that you publicly humiliate yourself with that lame schtick ten times a day on the tube but I'm not gonna have you doing any of that crap in here. Now go and fix me a vodka gimlet."

"Sure, baby, sure. Coming right up! I'll make this one extra special for you!"

"Just try and get it in the glass, will you, Frank?"

"Anything you say, baby."

So, this was Frank. Hard to believe that Krazy Kilgore, owner of the largest used car dealership in the quad city area, was, in reality, a submissive house boy who hopped to for Mistress Mansfield like a fraternity pledge during Hell Week. Hard to believe and even harder to watch. I quickly shifted my focus to Lacey who had kicked back on the sofa. After all, she was the one I'd come to talk to and now that she had slipped into a granny dress with glasses to match, I'd be able to do it face to face without her body butting in. Seeing as how she was such an earth mama, I decided to back off from the usual Joe Friday line of questioning and go for a Mod Squad vibe. That way I wouldn't seem so much like "The Man."

"Happening pad you've got here, Ms. Mansfield," I said sinking into a piece of cartoon furniture, "Trippy. Real trippy."

"You dig it, huh?" she said, looking around at the

mondo motif, "Well, if my old man were still alive, that would make two of you. He really got off on it. I always told him it symbolized the obscene excess of the corrupt ruling class, but he never listened to me. He went ahead and built the thing anyway. And now I'm stuck with it."

"If you hate it that bad, why don't you move?"

"Who would buy it? Besides, all his creepy little groupies would riot if I tried to sell this place. They claim he's going to reincarnate himself here as, I don't know, a cow or something. I try not to pay any attention to them. They're really whacked."

"Groupies? What was he? Some kind of big deal rock star?"

"Oh, no. Nothing that cool. You ever heard of *ept*?"

"Eichman Positivity Training? Sure. It was part of that Personal Enlightenment Movement that swept South Florida in the mid-seventies. Supposed to expand your mind and that kind of junk. Some self-proclaimed Nazi guru started it. People would shell out a couple of grand just to spend a weekend being screamed at by a sadist who told them what miserable losers they were while they sat in metal folding chairs for thirty-six hours without being allowed to eat, sleep or go to the bathroom. Real enlightening. I remember there were a bunch of low rent celebrities who signed up for that garbage. What happened? Your husband get suckered into that hustle?"

"No, he was the Nazi guru who started it."

"Your husband was Dieter Eichman?"

"Yeah, at least that's who he was to that flock of masochistic sheep that followed him around.

To me he was just Eddie. It used to really burn him when I called him that. He was such a jerk."

"Why'd you call him Eddie?"

"Cause that was his name, man. Eddie Mansfield. He changed it when he started *ept*. Nobody was gonna lay down their bread to listen to some used car salesman named Eddie tell them how to achieve total consciousness, so he came up with the name Dieter Eichman. After that, he grew sideburns, hung some beads around his neck and all of a sudden, everyone believed he was this New Age prophet with the magic formula to maximize human potential. All he really did was maximize his profits, the lyin' weasel."

"You're telling me that a guy who had thousands of people running around chanting and staring into the sun, peddled used cars?"

"You got it, Ace," said Frank throwing in his two scents while delivering Lacey's cocktail, "He was the best. I worked with him for years. Could sell ice cubes to an Eskimo. Best I ever saw."

She shot him a look that could pierce armor. Might even come close to going through that gut of his.

"Real jerk, though," Frank added quickly before tucking his ample tail between his thick legs and waddling back to his place behind the bar, "Never liked him. A rat bag all the way."

"Doesn't sound like the guru practiced what he preached."

"No, man, that's exactly what he did. 'Get Yours!' was the ten-cent catch phrase he used to lay on his dim bulb disciples. 'Get Yours!' Well, you better believe he got his. The thing was, he usually got it with one of those bouncy-bottomed usherettes that rounded up the cattle at his seminars. There were always three or four of them hangin' around. He even died with one of them."

"How'd that happen?"

"He was headed for a low rent motel out on Montauk Island to get it on with one of his bimbos when he lost control of the car and drove off a bridge. Both of them drowned. The cops say his brakes went out but I think it was because something else was out. It was when they found him, anyway. I had him buried like that, too."

"Sounds like he definitely 'got his' in the end. You know, speaking of accidents, that's the reason I wanted to come and talk with you. Daisy's had some close calls over the past couple of weeks and I'm trying to find out who's been ringing her up. I thought you might be able to help me put a trace on their line."

She took a healthy sip from her limed drink and gave Frank a quick glance before she came back with an answer.

"Daisy's always been, like, this beautiful free spirit, man. So in touch with everything and really together. You know, just groovin' along. Then she hooks up with this young unprogressive and from what she told me this morning, all of a sudden it's one bad scene after another. She's never had to deal with this kind of scary trip before and I can think of only one reason that she is now. It's him, man. It's that baby-faced fascist. He's got this really bad vibe happening. That's what's bringing all of this down on her. It's him."

"Like him, do you?"

"I'm just tellin' it like it is, man. Look, I don't get off on puttin' him down. I mean, I'm all for spreading peace and love and cosmic oneness and all that, but let's face it, he's nothing but an elitist droog from a family of depraved Establishment types who've poisoned his mind with their spiritually void, morally bankrupt, plutocratic dogma. And I don't want him corrupting Daisy with the same bigoted concepts."

"Can't you just put the kibosh on the wedding? You know, regardless of how you feel about the mother-daughter thing, you're still in position to exercise some authority over the situation."

"I couldn't oppress her like that, man. It would go against everything she thinks I believe in and I don't want to risk damaging her image of me. All I can do is meditate and keep chanting my mantra. I just hope it'll help open her eyes to that little goosestepper's rotten aura."

"Maybe she will open her eyes but, in the meantime, I'm trying to keep someone from puttin' pennies on them. Is there anything you could tell me that you think might help me out?"

"If there was, I'd tell you, man. It would be a real downer if something happened to Daisy. And, hey man, I dig the fact that you want to make sure everyone's mellow and all that, but I think you'll be wasting your time with all this Dick Tracy stuff. She just needs to get away from that piggy boyfriend and his warped clan. If she does that, she'll be cool. It's Karma, man. I'm tellin' you, it's all Karma."

If it was all Karma, then the kind that existed between Lacey Mansfield and Felicity Crisp was all bad. These two made Montague and Capulet look like Ricardo and Mertz. After hearing both of them spit venom that would make a snake handler cringe, Daisy's line about their mothers having a hard time getting used to the idea of the wedding seemed like a bit of an under-statement. How those two kids ever got together in the first place was a mystery to me, but I was trying to figure out a bigger one. Who was trying to stop this wedding and start a funeral? Since I hadn't grabbed any real leads from either of the moms, I was going to have to look elsewhere. Where elsewhere was, I didn't have a clue but it sure wasn't here. It was time to do my closing number and split.

"Well, like they say, *your mother should know*," I grunted as I tried to escape from that butt cuff of a chair I was sitting in, "And you may very well be right, Ms. Mansfield. It could be the result of some weird psychic chemistry going on between Daisy and Colin that's causing all of this trouble. I remember seeing an 'Outer Limits' where that happened. But just in case it's not, I'm sorta gonna do my own thing and keep checkin' out the scene because you're definitely right about one thing. It would be a real downer if something happened to either one of them."

"Whatever turns you on, man, but I think you'll be wasting your time. Like I said, as soon as that Crisp kid is out of her life, there'll be no more hassle. It'll be cool then."

It was like déjà vu all over again. I was getting the same reaction from Ms. Crisp. Neither of them seemed to think their kids were in any real danger nor did they feel there was any real need for my services. What they cared about most were appearances. They were afraid this proposed marriage would affect their social or in Lacey's case, anti-social standing in the community. Couldn't exactly recommend them, either one of them, for Mother of the Year. Kind of sad. I don't know what it feels like to have a kid but if one of my little soldiers ever broke ranks and took a hill, I like to think I'd have a tad more concern for the little ankle biter's well-being than these two birds.

"Let's hope it is, regardless. Anyway, pleasure meeting you, ma'am. It's been a real gas."

As I started to go, I saw Frank leaning on the bar with a glazed look on his ruddy face. I couldn't resist jerkin' his chain one last time before I left.

"See you on the tube, Frank!"

He hesitated for a second before snapping to, like a hippo coming out of hypnosis.

"Huh? Oh yeah! Be seein' you, pardner! And don't forget what we say down at Kilgore's Klassic Kars! We're committed to. . . "

"Frank! Your giving me a sick headache!" screamed Lacey, nipping him in his bulging bud.

"Later," I laughed as I hit the door. It was good to be getting out of there. I'd had about all the hippie-speak I could handle for one day. Between the sights and the sounds of Chéz Mansfield, I was ready to burn some fast rubber back to the city but not before I had a look-see at Frank's GTO. He may have been a disgusting sight, but his ride was a knockout. I was going to do the showroom circle once, then book. As I walked around the back of the car, I didn't pay much attention to the red and white license plate. Frank was a dealer, so he had a dealer's tag. Big deal. The fact that it was mounted crooked didn't jump out at me either. A lot of those plates were magnetic so they could be interchanged between cars for test drives and such, and this one was probably one of those. Again, no big deal. But then, I noticed something that was a big deal. Like a royal flush from

a seven-deck boot. The license number read DVL-666.
Three sixes on a dealer's plate. A dealer's plate like the
one on the Chevy that had tried to run down Colin last
night. A Chevy like the one Frank had talked about. And
Frank takes care of everything. It was him. It had to be.

I realized I had only seen the last three numbers
on the tag but there were way too many coincidences for
it to be anyone else. Plus, he had a motive. He knew that
Lacey was violently opposed to the marriage and that
nothing would make her happier than seeing it called
off. He also knew you can't have a wedding if you don't
have a groom, so he had decided to knock the little man
off the top of the cake. Being the groveling stooge that
he was, he must have figured this would put him in her
good books to stay. What he didn't know was that I was
going to edit out his chapter. But before I did anything,
I had to warn the kids. Until I could arrange to put
Kilgore out of commission, Colin would still be in danger and I wanted him to be on guard in case that corpu-
lent creep tried again. That's why I had to tell them the
truth. It was going to be tough, especially for Daisy, but
this was real life and they were going to have to face the
fact that sometimes real life really reeks. Sorry, Virginia,
there is no Santa Claus. There's no Easter Bunny, no
Tooth Fairy, and no happily ever after's. At least not in
St. Vegas.

It was time to go dump a bucket of coal under
their tree.

Chapter 4

I couldn't believe it. I was back on Sedgewick Avenue. When I called Colin to set up a meeting with him and Daisy, he suggested The Smoke & Caffeine Hookah Bar, one of those trendy water pipe bistros that I loathed so well. He said it was their favorite hangout and I thought it would be a good idea to break the news about Kilgore in a place where they'd feel at least some comfort. I hoped they would because I sure wasn't feeling any. Sitting in a booth that was covered with cigarette burns and patches of duct tape, I surveyed this sorry scene. It was two in the afternoon and the joint was full of goateed slackers and bohemian artistes downing double shots of espresso and counting each other's body piercings. Definitely not my crowd. I tried to tune them out while I waited for my young clients by pulling in my antennae and drinking a cup of mud while silently staring down at the table. Someone had scratched the word "sphincter" on it. Nice.

By the time Daisy and Colin showed up, I was on my third cup and my last nerve. This bunch of avant-garde art-farters was really starting to chap me. After being forced to listen to all these pinheads wheeze poetic for almost twenty minutes, I had decided my tête-á-tête with the kids was going to have to be a quick one. This hep cat-mosphere had gotten to me. So had the java. Best if I didn't hang too long. I just might blow. It would be best for them, too. Distressing news like this should be delivered in a simple, matter of fact style. Cut and dry. Short and sweet. Well, short anyway.

They sat down across from me holding hands, waiting in nervous anticipation for the results of my investigation. I hadn't given them any indication of what to expect so this was going to be a sucker punch to their psyches, not to mention their wedding plans. Looking across the table at their innocent, trusting faces, I could see this wasn't going to be as easy as I thought, but I couldn't hold this sick smile much longer without looking like the village idiot. I had to go ahead and tell them. I took a long, deep breath and began.

"Well. . . "

I had barely started speaking when a loud ping of metal on metal rang out beside us as a large brass plate hanging on the wall next to Daisy crashed onto our table. Less than a second later my coffee mug exploded in my hand. Colin jumped to protect Daisy and when he did, he bumped into a waiter who was carrying a large dessert tray that went flying right into a busboy with a tub full of dirty mugs. The busboy tripped and dumped the tub on two tables full of overly caffeinated customers who fell out of their chairs, slipping and sliding on a giant coffee slick, bringing about a chaotic chain reaction that spread throughout the entire cafe. It was like watching a life-sized game of Mousetrap. What's worse, I was still hearing those sharp pings bouncing around us. The place was like a café au lait combat zone. I had to get Daisy and Colin out of there. Taking one underneath each wing, I headed for the door, ducking and dodging through the barrage of demitasse missiles and whipped cream land mines exploding around us in this battlefield brasserie.

After I shuffled the young ones to safety, I peeked back inside to try and figure out what just happened in there. One look was all it took. Sheltered at a back table, conspicuously inconspicuous while sliding a miniature glass blowgun from his spritzer to his pocket, was that anorexic worm, Norman J. Nance. This changed everything.

Chapter 5

itting at my office desk flipping through an old copy of Argosy while the six o'clock news provided a little TV ambience, I wondered how I could have been such a sap not to have seen that Nance was in this. I should have realized it the second I found out Kilgore was involved. He was every bit the favor-seeking sycophant that greasy chunk of bovine blubber was, it's just that he was on the other side. They were both attempting to elevate their status with their respective boss ladies by having Daisy's and Colin's lowered. Six feet under to be exact. Now that they knew I was poking around, there was no doubt they'd step it up a notch and try to dispose of them in quick fashion. Nance had already proven that. My problem was figuring out a way to take both of them out with one shot. It would be too risky to go after them one at a time because while I was collaring one, the other could get lucky and score a bullseye and I didn't want either of them taking home a Kewpie doll from this carnival. This was going to be all or nothing. I chose the former.

Knowing those two asinine assassins wouldn't be would-be enough to risk getting caught on enemy turf, I felt the safest place for Daisy and Colin was in their own homes, so I told them to go there and stay. I also told them not to say anything about what happened at the cafe. In fact, it was best they not say anything to anyone. Just stay in their rooms. Fake a migraine or a bellyache if they had to, but above all, keep to themselves and don't leave the house. I said I had an idea about what was causing these accidents and that I was going to try and stop it. They were to call me at my office at noon the next day. If I didn't answer, that meant something went wrong and they should immediately call Lt. Deke Dombrowski at police headquarters and tell him everything. That about covered it. Except for one thing. I didn't tell them about Kilgore and Nance. I was afraid they might wig out and accidentally spill the beans to one or both of those jerks before I could devise a plan to end their little reign of error. Exactly what that plan was, I didn't know yet. Maybe I'd get an idea from one of the articles in this magazine. "I Was A Teenage G-Man." "Death Eats A Cracker." "Hot Chicks On A Cold Slab." Well, maybe not.

I was in the middle of reading an ad for an electric nose shaver when a news story caught my ear and took my eye along with it to the television. They were reporting that former Crabs relief pitcher and Skivvies underwear model Louie LeCoat had been arrested last night by St. Vegas police on charges of grand larceny, illegal gambling and conspiracy to commit mayhem. The report also stated that an unnamed civilian accomplice was believed to have been instrumental in helping police capture LeCoat. However, a department spokesman would neither confirm nor deny this part of the story. Gee, wonder who it could be? Seeing LeCoat screaming "I'll get you, Wilder!" into the camera may have tipped a couple of people off, but since I wasn't exactly what you'd call a household name in this town, I wasn't expecting any personal congrats from the mayor or homemade pies from the Ladies Auxiliary. Anyway, it looked like Ol' Louie was pretty upset. Guess he's allergic to stings.

Wait a minute. That was it. That was how I'd get Nance and Kilgore. With a sting. I'd use a variation of the old Saratoga Double Dutch. Play two ends against the middle, they cancel each other out and you take the bundle. I've seen it worked to such perfection that the marks never even knew what hit them. It wasn't going to be played that close to perfect this time, though. I wanted these two pinheads to know what hit them. Webb Wilder.

Chapter 6

The Bull and China Shop was an upscale emporium on the west side that catered to the local snobbery and specialized in fine china and crystal along with excessive amounts of delicate porcelain geegaws that inevitably found their way to the gift tables of countless brides registered by overbearing mothers. It was owned by my Uncle Frank who had retired from a semi-lucrative import/export business in Speonk, New York, to live out the rest of his days in this quaint little shop where he could supplement his social security while he ogled young girls. He was happy and the shop was doing well. So well, in fact, that he was able to close it up on Wednesdays and go drinkin' and drivin' out on the links at the St. Vegas country club. This Wednesday, however, the shop would be open, but only for two very special customers who were going to learn the meaning of caveat emptor. Let the buyer beware.

It took three rehearsals and a couple of

Venn diagrams to make sure this scam would run but I finally got it down. The set up went off without a hitch. I had called the Mansfield residence figuring that idiot Kilgore would be doing his Jeeves imitation so I knew that he would be the one to answer the phone. I told him I had an appointment to meet Daisy and Colin that morning at the Bull and China Shop to discuss the case while they registered for wedding gifts. I said I had spoken with Daisy about it the night before and told her I wasn't going to be able to make it, but I hadn't been able to get in touch with Colin to tell him. I didn't want him to be there all alone so I asked if he could please have Daisy inform Colin that the meeting was off. He said, "No problem, pardner!" and I could almost hear him salivating as he hung up the phone. I then immediately called the gallery and laid the same spiel on Nance, only with the roles reversed. He was to have Colin tell Daisy about the change of plans. "Certainly, Mr. Wilder. It will be my pleasure." That's what you think, scarecrow.

The desired result of this scheme was for these pigeons to not say a word about the calls. Instead, they would come to the shop, each thinking they were going to have a clear shot at their target without having to worry about the home team being in the line of fire. It was an opportunity they couldn't pass up. They'd be there, alright. And so would I.

It was a few ticks before ten in the a.m. when I arrived at the shop with my game face already on. For this particular ruse, I had chosen to assume the guise of Lyle, the crusty but benign shopkeeper. He fit the surroundings and would easily fool Kilgore and Nance. He also fit my budget. A comb-over and set of novelty teeth pretty much did it. I was in the back room adjusting my uppers when I heard the front door jingle open. One chump was here. I had been wondering who was going to be the first to show. Earlier, for amusement only of course, I had handicapped this race. When I shuffled out onto the main floor, I saw I had picked a winner because standing there, in a natty, well-pressed delivery boy's uniform accented with a paisley ascot, was my little Normie. It was showtime.

"Deliveries are around back, fella! How many times do I have to tell you guys?"

"I beg your pardon?"

"See? That's your problem right there!" I griped in a transplanted Midwestern brogue, "You guys don't listen when somebody's talkin' to ya. If ya did, ya'd know that all deliveries are around back!"

"No, you don't understand. I'm not. . . "

"No, by Godfrey, *you* don't understand! Deliveries are around back! I can't seem to stress that enough!"

"Apparently not," sighed Nance, trying hard to maintain his composure, "but, sir, if you will allow me, please. I am not here to make a delivery to you."

"What are ya doin' then? Loafin'? That's what's wrong with this country today! This younger set doesn't wanna work! All they wanna do is zoom up and down the boulevard in their hot rods, drinkin' pop and listenin' to that Be-Bop music on the radio and it's sending this country straight to Hell! I tell ya, it makes ya just wanna rip out your spleen and feed it to a badger, ya know?"

It took a moment for that one to register with him.

"Ah, yes, of course. Out with the old spleener. Most certainly. However, as I told you, I have not come to deliver a package to you but rather, to a young lady who I was told would be in your shop at about this time."

"Well, as you can see, she ain't in here. Say, did ya check around back? Could be she's waitin' on you out there. That's where deliveries are made, ya know."

"No, I did not and that is because, my dear fellow, it was my understanding that the young lady would be coming to your place of business to prepare a registry for her wedding. Call me presumptuous but I did not believe that I would find her doing so on your back dock!"

"Oh, no, she wouldn't be doin' that back there. That's for. . . "

"Don't say it!"

Beautiful. Nance was getting steamed, which was exactly how I wanted him. I just had to keep him going until Kilgore showed. I'd give Big Boy a heavy dose of the same, then sic them on each other and watch the fun begin. Didn't look like I was going to have to wait too long for the fireworks to start, either. A large, round figure had just caused a total eclipse in the shop's door-way. Krazy, man, Krazy.

Wobbling in like the weebil he was, Kilgore entered wearing a plaid driving cap and a brown bomber jacket with worn elbows and a TCB patch sewn on the sleeve. He looked like an extra from the set of "Taxi" which, it turned out, was what he was going for.

"Excuse me there, pardner. I'm here to. . . "

"Make a delivery?"

"Dear God, please. Not again," I heard Nance plead under his breath.

"Cause if you are, I'll tell ya the same thing I told him. Deliveries are around back! I guess I'm going to have to put up a darn neon sign or somethin' before you guys get it right. Criminy!"

"No, no. I'm not making any deliveries. I'm here to pick up a fare."

"A what?"

"A fare. You know, a ride?"

"Oh, I can't give you no ride, buddy. I gotta watch the store."

"No, no, no. I'm here to give one to someone else."

"Well, that's awful nice of you, friend but, like I said, I can't leave the store. Maybe this fella here'll take you up on it."

"No, no, no, no. Listen to me. I am a cab driver. I am supposed to be picking up someone from your shop. He called and said this was where he would be."

"Maybe it was him," I said pointing to Nance.

"No, it wasn't him! It was some kid!"

"Could have been one of them crank calls, ya know. Those little wisenheimers are always callin' down here tryin' to pull their shenanigans on me. 'May I speak to Phil, please? Phil who? Miaz. Phil Miaz? Feel yer own ass, ya rotten kids!' I swear, I'm gonna get those little buggers one day."

"Oh, for the love of God, man!" exploded Nance, "Will you please stop dilly-dallying about with this blasted coachman and pay attention to me!"

Kilgore didn't take too kindly to Nance's outburst.

"Hey, I was talkin' here, Twiggy."

"I believe I was holding the floor long before you arrived, you unmannered clod!"

"Keep poppin' wise to me and you're gonna be on

the floor, pantywaist!"

"Lay a hand on me and you shall regret it, blatherskite!"

"Wait a minute, now, fellas," I interjected, "I can't have no scufflin' in the store. Just settle down and let me see if I can't help the both of ya out there. Now, you there, you're lookin' for a young girl, right? And Cabbie, with you it's a boy. Hmm. Ya know, it seems like there were two kids in here earlier. Boy and a girl. Yeah, I remember now. Nice kids. Said a couple of guys would be coming by looking for them and to give them this message. You're busted!"

That was my cue to spit out the fake choppers and flip my brimmed personality out from under the counter and back on my head. To say the least, the boys were surprised. And in stereo.

"Wilder!"

"Norm! Frankie, baby! My two favorite schmucks! How're they hangin', boys?"

From the looks on their faces, I expected to hear a duet of "Homina, homina, homina" kick in at any second.

"Oh, come on, guys. Admit it. You knew it was me, didn't you? Cause, you know, I knew it was you all along. I mean, Frank, using the same license plate? Not too smooth, pardner. And Norman, you with that pea shooter attack at the cafe yesterday. Ferns and brass rails just don't provide adequate camouflage in that kind of combat situation, soldier. Add to those bits of evidence a couple of kowtowing lackeys who'd do anything to seek favor from their queens and you'll see that I didn't have to jump very high to reach this conclusion."

Not being quick studies, they weren't really

catching my drift. They just stood there, each doing a series of baffled takes from me back to their witless counterpart.

"You seem a little confused, fellas. Let me try and explain this thing to you. You see, Frank, Norman here works for Felicity Crisp. I'm sure you're familiar with her. She's Colin's mother. Colin, I'm sure you're aware, is the young man you've been trying to flatten with all those attempted hit-and-runs. And, Norman, you're not going to believe this, but Frank is the boyfriend slash doormat of Lacey Mansfield who, as you know, is Daisy's mom. I just think that's so ironic since you've been doing your best to bump Daisy off. Life's funny, huh?"

Their confusion immediately turned to rage when they realized they were in the presence of the enemy. This, of course, meant war.

"So you've been plotting to do away with young Colin, have you?" shouted Nance at the top of his puny lungs, "I'll do you for that, ya bleeda!"

"Bring it on, you Limey pansy!" Kilgore shot back, "I'll teach you to try and hurt a little girl. I'm gonna knock them crooked teeth down your skinny throat!"

"In a pig's eye, you overstuffed Iago! Nothing will stop me from preventing that foul strumpet from blackening the Crisp family name by forcing our lad into marriage!"

"Well, you're outta your freakin' mind if you think I'm gonna let that snot-nose punk take Daisy away from her mother. That little creep ain't even good enough for her to spit on!"

"I'll eliminate you and that little trollop, you rotter!"

"Wrong, girlie man! It's me who's takin' the both of you out!"

"Cut! Print! Beautiful!" I said holding up a mini camcorder, "That was perfect, gentleman. This video ought to play real well at the trial. The judge is going to love it. Well, I guess that's a wrap. Thanks for coming. This has been a Webb Wilder production."

I had caught them red handed and red faced. They looked back and forth trying to decide who to go for to get out of this trap. It was like the stand-off in "The Good, the Bad and the Ugly." Of course, they were the ugly. Finally, they made their choice. Kilgore picked me and Nance chose Kilgore. Let's get ready to rumble!

Before Fat Frank could make it to the counter where I was standing, Nance shot across the floor and jumped on his back like Sabu on a circus elephant. The two crashed into a wall of shelving and smashed an entire collection of glass figurines as they both fell to the floor. Kilgore then got up with Nance still hanging on to his neck like an anemic pit bull and started bucking and spinning around the store, trying in vain to throw off his unwanted papoose. I stood back and watched them thrash about thinking it was a pretty funny sight, which it was, until I realized they were completely destroying Uncle Frank's shop. He wasn't going to be too pleased with the way it was being redecorated so I figured I'd best put a stop to this melee, toot sweet.

I jumped the counter like a burly bouncer in a bar fight and ran over to separate them, but I couldn't get a good hold on either of the two. Kilgore was still spinning, and Nance was still riding but the big fella finally got too dizzy and stopped with his fop-laden back facing the front door. They were both panting like a couple of puckered pooches in August with Nance's head sitting atop Kilgore's like faces on a totem pole. This was my chance to adjourn this meeting before they made another motion. I carefully measured Kilgore's chin, then placed a floor-dragging uppercut right on it. The top of his head relayed the punch to Nance's jaw, which sent him flying off Kilgore's back and out the display window. Frank's bulbous butt then crashed through the front door and onto the sidewalk. They were both out like lights. Mission accomplished. I really had them both with one shot.

As I walked to the phone to call for the paddy wagon, I took a look around the shop to assess the damage. They had literally broken and smashed everything in the place. Everything except a small porcelain bull sitting on a little glass pedestal. Oh, the bitter irony. Still, it was the perfect spot to leave a note of explanation for Uncle Frank. "Sorry about the mess. Somebody sneezed. Hope you're covered. See you next Christmas. W.W."

The desk sergeant at the station answered my call.

"Third Precinct. Sgt. Habeñero."

"Yeah, tell Dombrowski there's a couple of packages waiting for him at the Bull and China Shop on Fourth and Long. And make sure he knows to pick them up out front. Deliveries are around back."

Chapter 7

With Fat Man and Little Boy diffused, it appeared the case was wrapped, but something told me this package wasn't ready for a ribbon just yet. Something was missing. After seeing Nance and Kilgore in action, I knew there was no way those two meatheads could have acted on their own. Somebody else was directing this foul play and it was pretty obvious who those somebodies were. I didn't want to believe it myself, so before I laid anything that heavy on Colin and Daisy, I needed proof. Clear cut proof. Proof that would pull me out of doubt's shadow needing a pair of shades. I figured the best place to start was with the kids. Maybe they knew a reason why their mothers hated each other enough to have their flunkies do a contract job on their children. When they called at noon, I would have them come in, ask them a few questions and see if I couldn't get to the bottom of this family feud without either one catching on to this sordid soap opera. Not as easy as it sounded. With kids, it's the eyes, man. It's hard to lie to those eyes.

They called within seconds of each other and I could tell that just hearing my voice on the phone was a big relief to both of them. Being asked to come to the office made them feel even better since they assumed that their leaving the house meant everything was okay. I wanted them to keep thinking that way for as long as they could or at least until I gave them good reason not to. They made it there in less than an hour and sat down in front of my desk with an anxious look, like they were waiting for the results of cheerleader tryouts. Jeez, this was going to be tough.

"First of all, you can stop worrying about any more weird accidents coming your way. You were right. It was just coincidence. Nothing to worry about at all."

"Great!" whewed Colin, "I thought that's all it was, but I have to admit, after what happened in the cafe yesterday, I was starting to wonder."

"Me, too," added Daisy, "That was so bizarre. I've never seen anything like that before, have you?"

"Only on an episode of 'Three's Company,'" I told her, "but, like I said, forget all that stuff. It's over and done with. I do, though, want to talk to you about something else that's bothering me a little bit. When I talked to your moms, I came away with the impression that they don't like each other. I mean, they *really* don't like each other. Do either of you know what that's all about?"

"Well, sorta," said Daisy meekly, "It was something that happened a long time ago when they were in school together." "You know what she's talking about, Colin?"

"Yeah. The thing with the doll."

"Tell me about it."

They did. And as I listened, I started to understand why these two women were the way they were. I started to understand a lot of things. Some, I think I would have been better off not knowing.

The following, translated into Webbanese, is what they told me.

* * * * * * *

In October of nineteen sixty-three, St. Hubbins Academy, a private parochial school for young girls, was in the middle of their annual Harvest Festival, a gala celebration promoting fellowship and culminating with the highlight of the week's activities, the Little Miss Orange Blossom Pageant. Each year, parents and teachers alike looked forward to seeing the students display their talents in this always entertaining exhibition of budding charm and grace. Although held under the auspices of good-natured competition and camaraderie, the pageant had become a highly contested event with some mothers working all summer coaching their daughters on their performance. However, this year's competition would prove to be more intense than ever before because, along with the crown, the winner would also be presented with an advance release, special edition Barbie doll. The doll, created in honor of the country's trendsetting First Lady, was donated to the school by the man who designed it. A man who also happened to be the brother of the school's pastor, Father Poe. There was talk that the donation was really an act of atonement by the prodigal brother for leaving the seminary years earlier to pursue a career in miniature fashion design but regardless of the rumors, the doll was highly prized and the pageant, highly anticipated. There was no doubt that the little girls of St. Hubbins would go all out to capture the plastic teen-age fashion model.

Once the competition began, there were the conventional piano pieces, baton twirlings, dramatic readings and show tunes. But in a year that saw not one, but two renditions of "Theme from a Summer Place" played on the recorder, the performances of two contestants stood above all the rest. Two little girls whose talents were unmatched and whose drive and determination were unequaled. They were two little girls named Felicity and Lacey.

After easily eliminating all of the other pintsized participants, these two eight-year-old performing dynamos and lifelong best friends were left to go head-to-head in a "sudden death" show-off. And show off they did. They pulled out all the stops. Singing, dancing, performing grand illusions, composing extemporaneous haiku. If it had been Friday, they probably would have done the miracle of the loaves and fishes. As the competition escalated to a fever pitch with the crowd on the edge of their collective seat, the little troupers performed at such dizzying heights heretofore seen only in the championship round of "Ted Mack's Original Amateur Hour." Back and forth it went like a classic ring battle. It was Lamotta-Robinson. It was Ali-Frazier. It was actually like Mary-Kate and Ashley competing for Daddy's attention on Father's Day. No fiercer competition than that.

Finally, with the crowd completely spent and gasping for breath, the contestants sweating like

Sammy Davis, Jr. during his third set at the Copa and the judges unable to pick a winner, Father Poe stepped forth and mercifully proclaimed the contest a draw. He said that both of the girls deserved to win but since there was only one grand prize, there would have to be a compromise. They would have to share the doll. This shouldn't be too difficult to work out, he said, especially since the girls were such good friends.

While Felicity and Lacey posed side by side with Father Poe in pictures for the *Daily Trombone*, their friendship had already started to take a backseat to self-interest as each held on to the doll, pulling on it like two livid lumberjacks on a double handled timber saw. These were just shades of things to come.

It was grudgingly agreed that the girls would each keep the doll on alternating weeks. With a week seeming like six months when you're that age plus the fact that neither of these kids were any great shakes when it came to sharing, problems naturally arose. If the one girl whose week it was brought the doll for show and tell, there was inevitably a fight between the two. The now former friends were constantly bickering and would continually disrupt class with their loud arguments. Their teachers, unable to handle the situation, had turned it over to Miss Gulch, the school principal, a tough old battleax who ran the academy like a warden in a women's prison. She would handle these little hellcats with no problem. At least that's what they all thought until she stepped into the middle of one of Felicity and Lacey's punch-outs and came away with the worst of it. That was enough for her. It was time to go and see the pastor.

Father Alan Poe was a kind, grandfatherly old priest whose combination of erudite wisdom and gentle, caring demeanor had made him the most beloved figure at the school for over forty years. By applying his calm, thoughtful logic, he had solved many a problem that had come his way in that time. Mrs. Gulch, bursting into his office carrying Felicity and Lacey by the scruff of their necks while they each held on tight to one of their precious Barbie's legs, was about to provide him with one of his more difficult dilemmas.

"Father," said Mrs. Gulch as she dumped the girls into the two chairs in front of the pastor's desk, "We have a serious problem with our little pageant queens. They have been throwing this school into complete and total turmoil with their fighting and arguing over this doll. They have been scolded, put in detention and have even felt the sting of a ruler on their palms but to no avail. We are all at our absolute wit's end trying to find a way to deal with these two. I didn't know of any other solution, so we've come to you. I don't like taking up your valuable time with matters such as this, but it's become more than any of us can handle!"

"Well now, Mrs. Gulch, I think we can solve this problem without getting upset and resorting to such stern measures. Right, girls?"

The girls sat stone faced, staring at the floor while still clutching the doll.

"Come now, girls. You've been friends much too long for something like this to come between you. Friendship is a precious gift and not something to be taken lightly. It's far more valuable than any plastic dolly. If you will just try to share that Barbie doll like you've shared your friendship for the last four years,

I think you'll understand what I'm saying and you'll stop all of this silly bickering. After all, it doesn't make you feel very good inside, does it?"

Still no response.

"Alright, now. Felicity. Lacey. Look at me. Look right here and tell me that you're going to stop all this nonsense and share the doll like we agreed. Is that what we're going to do?"

Still, defiant silence.

"Girls, we can't keep disrupting class over a doll. A doll!" The pastor's tone was becoming firmer. "You must share!"

Finally, an answer came.

"No!"

Father Poe sat with his hands folded in front of his face while he contemplated his response. After a moment, he delivered it. Swiftly.

"Well then, girls," he said rising from his chair, "You leave me no choice."

He quickly reached over his desk and snatched the doll from out of their hands and held it high above his head as a near demonic look came over his once winsome face. Pointing down at the two frightened waifs like Heston damning Edward G. Robinson's myrrhzola party after coming down off the mountain with the Commandments, the possessed pastor spoke in a somewhat different tone.

"Look upon your treachery, vile sinners! Heareth the words of Solomon and despair! 'He that troubleth his own house shall inherit the wind'! Girls, follow me and learn the pain of contempt and idolatry."

The priest bounded from his desk and out of his office door. The two girls were hustled behind him by the prodding of Mrs. Gulch, following with a mix of dread and wonder at what was next. The school hallways quickly turned from the cheerful colors of displayed class projects to the roughhewn stone and dirt floor of the school basement. The pastor's determined walk finally ended in the janitor's workshop. The girls, panting and out of breath from the breakneck walk to the bowels of the building, looked on in terror as the priest turned quickly on his heels to continue his sermon. Again, Father Poe held up the doll, hitting her against one of the bare light bulbs hanging from the ceiling.

"And the king said, 'Bring me a sword'!"

As he pointed to the corner work bench, Mrs. Gulch picked up on the cue and handed him a dusty hacksaw.

"And they brought the king a sword!"

He now stood the doll on the bench with his hand wrapped tightly around its waist while he waved the hacksaw over its plastic noggin.

"And the king said, 'Divide the living child in two, and give half to one, and half to the other'!"

With that, as Felicity and Lacey watched in horror, he took the hacksaw, placed it on top of the doll's head and began cutting it in half. He added some chanting for effect while Mrs. Gulch looked on with demented delight.

"Yibbidi, bobbadi, bobbadi, bah! Saliatseah, saliatseah, corrunda, condaliatseah!"

When he had finished carving, the familiar look of calm returned to the pastor's face as he handed each girl one half of the new doll he had just created. Bilateral Barbie.

"Well, I think we've reached a pleasant compromise, don't you? Everything is once again as it should be. Good day girls and always remember the wisdom of Solomon. 'A merry heart maketh a cheerful countenance.' Now go in peace, young ones."

Mrs. Gulch steered the stunned students out of the workshop, each holding parts of what was once their prized doll while Father Poe leaned back in the janitor's chair with a contented smile and lit up his pipe. He may have solved one problem but another one that would prove to be a whole lot bigger had just been created.

* * * * * * *

"That is one wild tale," I said picking my jaw up off of my desk.

"It's no 'Cat in the Hat' that's for sure," said Colin, "When I was around eleven or twelve, I was rooting through some boxes in the attic and found an old diary of my mom's and that story was in there. I know I shouldn't have read it but once I started, I couldn't stop. It's a good thing too, because we would have never known about it. Neither one of our moms has ever mentioned it."

"So that display in your mother's office? That's the same doll?"

"Yeah, that's it. It's turned sideways like that so you can't see that it's been cut in half but it's the same doll."

"Daisy, did your mom keep her half?"

"Oh, yeah. She keeps it in her bedroom. It's the centerpiece to this really weird Woodstock diorama she made years ago in this creepy art class. Most everyone there was always stoned, and the instructor didn't wear pants. It was really gross."

After hearing all of this, I tried to think of a way to help these kids out. This had been a helluva thing for them to live with, not to mention what their moms had gone through. A small flicker of a light bulb went off in my head. Nothing big, just a hint of something that I thought might be able to erase all the years of pain and suffering and in the process, maybe reunite a couple of old friends.

"Listen, kids. I need you to do something for me. I need you to pick up a couple of things and bring them here to the office."

"Sure. What's up?" asked Colin.

"Have you two ever been to Saratoga?"

Chapter 8

L acey Mansfield arrived at the Hotel Cestadoré not really knowing what to expect. She hadn't recognized the voice that called and told her that, at four o'clock that afternoon, a private auction would be held in Suite 309 of the hotel with only one item up for bid. An original, one-of-a-kind prototype of the never released, nineteen sixty-three *First Lady* model Barbie doll. She didn't know how many people besides her knew about the auction, who would be there or how high they would bid. She did know one thing, however. No matter what it took, she was going to get that doll.

She had expected the room to be full of Barbie collectors from all over but upon entering the suite, she was surprised to find it completely empty. After double checking the room number, she went back inside and took a look around. Rather than the trademark Cestadoré opulence of fine antique furniture and elegant decor, there appeared to be a special set-up in this suite.

In the middle of the room was a large Victorian table with a single, hand carved mahogany box resting at its center. Directly in front of the table, were two matching chairs setting side by side and facing straight ahead. If this was where the auction was to be held, Lacey must have thought, it was sure going to be an exclusive one. Looked like she'd only be bidding against one other person. Great! That meant it was in the bag. There wasn't another person anywhere that would go as high or as far to win this doll. Nowhere but in this room. Felicity Crisp had just walked in.

They both stopped in their tracks and looked hard into each other's eyes. It wasn't combative or hostile. More like dazed and confused. Neither moved nor spoke. They just stood there. Shell-shocked by an overload of emotions. Not wanting either of them to blow a fuse, I decided to make my entrance.

"Good afternoon, ladies," I said taking my position behind the table, "If you'll please have a seat, we'll begin."

My sudden presence didn't break the spell, it just added to it. They slowly turned toward me like they were doing The Robot and gave me that empty Stepford Wives gaze. I needed to do something to snap them out of it. I thought I'd try a little Lewis.

"Hey, la-a-a-dies!"

I always knew what the French saw in him. It's nice to see that particular bit still works. Both of the mothers blinked back to some degree of consciousness and cautiously took a seat. I took a moment, then started my pitch.

"Ms. Crisp, Ms. Mansfield, or if I may, Felicity and Lacey. I've asked you here today because I felt I had no other choice. You see, I know what happened between you two all those years ago. And, while it was a terribly tragic episode in your young lives, it shouldn't have led to all this. To the pain and hurt that it's brought not only to you but to your loved ones, as well. It just shouldn't have gone this far. So, I think it's time to stop. Yes, stop the madness and realize that families and friendships are the most precious gifts you can ever have and that all life is priceless, nor can any be replaced."

John Bradshaw eat your heart out.

With that last line, I had their complete and undivided attention. Either that or they were in a coma. No matter. It was time to make my final play. A last-ditch effort to wash out the stains caused by this bad blood, leaving the clean, bright fabric of friendship to wave triumphantly on the clothesline of love. Here goes.

"Ladies, I realize you've come here looking to find something that you thought was lost forever. A doll. But I'm here to tell you that there's something much more valuable to be found here than any plastic doll, and it's sitting right next to you. Yes, that's right. It's your friendship! It's here for the taking, if only you can give it. Come on, what am I bid for a big ol' hug?"

As I driveled out that last line, I reached into the box and pulled out the results of a little plastic surgery I had performed that afternoon in my office. Held high above my head and joined together with some thread and a bottle of airplane glue, was Barbie. Their Barbie. The two were now one again. I hoped it would have the same effect on Felicity and Lacey.

They stared wide-eyed at the restored doll as I moved it closer to give them a better look.

Okay, so it wasn't quite good as new but that wasn't the point. I was trying to show them that, like this doll, their friendship could be put back together just as easily. Only hopefully a bit neater. I thought it was working, too. They looked at the Barbie, then at each other. I could see something in both of their eyes. I thought it might be a small glimmer of the feelings they had shared as young innocent schoolgirls, so long ago. Turned out to be raging insanity. They let out a couple of screams that would have scared off a rabid pitbull and dove for the doll. Before I could move, they had taken it out of my hand and were wrestling around on the floor trying to take it away from each other. There was clawing and biting and pulling hair and smashing up furniture all over the room. Normally, I love a good cat fight but this one was getting way out of hand, especially since I had signed for the room and these tables and chairs they were splintering didn't exactly come from Second Hand Charlie's. If I didn't want to go into hock for the next millennium, I was going to have to break this up. And I would have, too. It's just that, I remembered what happened to Mrs. Gulch when she tried to step in and if that leathery old hag couldn't take them when they were girls, I sure wasn't going to try and do it now that they were full grown women. They weren't taking any prisoners and I wasn't taking any chances. I made a hasty retreat out the door as the battle inside raged on. Foolhardy, I ain't.

Epilogue

Security had called the cops not long after the fight started so there were already three black and whites and two ambulances waiting in front of the hotel when I came out. So was Dombrowski. He was leaning against one of the cruisers, smoking a cigarette and flanked by his two badged Bobbsey twins. I walked over to meet him just as an antique couch crashed through a window of Suite 309 and landed in the street.

"You really have a way with the ladies, Wilder. What the hell did you start up there?"

"What's going on up there started a long time before I got involved. All I did was put a stop to it. Just not the way I intended."

"What was your original plan, then? Bazookas at twenty paces?"

A large chifforobe shattered another window and splintered on the sidewalk.

"Bazookas. Yeah. it probably should have been. Would've been a lot quieter."

"Well, I've got their valets in custody, charged with attempted murder, conspiracy and reckless endangerment. What about those two upstairs? Same thing?"

"No, they're guilty of a far worse crime."

"What's that?"

"Being bad mothers."

"You're right about that. They are a couple of bad mothers. I've got six of my men up there right now trying to take them down and I still may have to call for backup."

"If I were you, I wouldn't hesitate."

The sounds of destruction from Suite 309 had died down to where Dombrowski felt safe enough to go in himself. He and his attendants were headed inside when I looked up and saw that Daisy and Colin were headed toward me.

What could I say to them? My scheme to bring their moms back together had failed miserably. After bagging LeCoat and then Nance and Kilgore, I had gone for the three-peat and been swept in the final round. These kids had already lost their fathers and now, thanks to me, their mothers would be going away too. How could I explain? This was going to be rough but as they came closer, I decided to do like I was going to do before. Tell the truth. Although, I kind of doubted it was going to set me free this time. This burden of guilt was way too big of a load.

"Daisy, Colin, I don't know what to say. It's. . . I'm really. . . "

"Hey, man! You were great!" beamed Daisy.

"Yeah, Wilder," smiled Colin, "You were hellacious, man! You were able to do in two days what we've been trying to do for two years."

Smiles and gratitude? Something wasn't right here.

"What are you talking about?"

"Our moms, stupid," said Daisy, "For years, we tried to figure out how to put those lunatics away and then you came along and it all fell into place. I can't believe it! I am so stoked!"

Dombrowski and his boys looked a little worse for wear as they brought Felicity and Lacey out of the hotel kicking and screaming and placed them in separate ambulances. They were in strait jackets. Looked like Kilgore wasn't the only one who was crazy.

"Oh, yeah!" shouted Colin acting like he had just sunk the winning putt at *The Masters*, "They're off to the nut house for friggin' ever! And you know what that means, Daisy Dearest."

"You bet your skinny butt I do!" squealed Daisy, "We get the money! We get the money! Yes! Yes! Yes!"

As they performed a victory dance that made Deion Sanders look like Lou Gehrig, it started to become clear that these weren't the same two frightened waifs I had rescued two nights ago in The Boneyard. Hard to believe it had all been an act. I needed to look back at the program and see what I'd missed.

"Are you tellin' me that this was a set-up from the start?"

"Pretty much," said Colin, after a few more hugs and high fives, "Like we told you, we had been looking a long time for a way to get rid of those two nut cases and when we ran into you the other night, we figured you could do all of the work. You took care of everything. Wrapped it up, all neat and nice. It was a real kick watching you perform. Funny stuff, man."

I felt like I had just received a cleated kick below the belt.

"Oh, don't be like that," said Daisy condescendingly, "You did a good thing, you know. You got rid of a couple of murderers."

"Yeah, right," interrupted Colin, "Those dorks couldn't find their butts with both hands. I was worried they would wind up killing themselves before we could use them in this deal."

"Well, anyway," laughed Daisy, "You did manage to push both of our moms completely over the edge, which was just, like, the coolest."

"Not as cool as the fact that we're both loaded now," said Colin, "Which reminds me, we took care of the room for you, man. We figured it was the least we could do, which is all we were planning on doing. Heh-heh!"

Suppressing a strong urge to snap this punk's neck, I asked one last question.

"So, all of this was done just so you two could get married and live in style while your moms bounced around in a rubber room for the rest of their lives."

"Are you kidding?" asked Daisy scornfully "Get married? Screw that! Baby, I'm getting out of this crummy burg and going to live on a beach somewhere. Get married! You must be high!"

"Yeah, and besides, I'm gay," added Colin, "Later, dude."

Well, that about said it all. They were definitely not the same kids I had tried to protect. They were a couple of ruthless little Machiavelli's who had played everyone, including me, like three chord Country.

CPSIA information can be obtained
at www.ICGtesting.com
Printed in the USA
BVHW041609310821
615691BV00015B/484

9 781737 667506